RELENTLESS - AN ARRANGED MARRIAGE SCOTTISH MAFIA ROMANCE

The MacTavish Stolen Brides Series - Book One

Arianna Fraser

SLC, LLC

Copyright © 2024 STA, LLC

All rights reserved

The characters and events portrayed in this book are fictitious. Any similarity to real persons, living or dead, is coincidental and not intended by the author.

No part of this book may be reproduced, or stored in a retrieval system, or transmitted in any form or by any means, electronic, mechanical, photocopying, recording, or otherwise, without express written permission of the publisher.

ISBN-13: 9798882966781
ISBN-10: 1477123456

Cover design by: Art Painter
Library of Congress Control Number: 2018675309
Printed in the United States of America

To my utterly wonderful and demented husband. We've had our wedding vows renewed by Elvis in Las Vegas, the Fraser Castle in Scotland, at a lighthouse in Maine, and so, so many times at Burning Man.

Honey, every time we say, "I do," I want to marry you all over again.

CONTENTS

Title Page
Copyright
Dedication
Preface
Forward 1
Prologue 2
Chapter One 3
Chapter Two 9
Chapter Three 12
Chapter Four 19
Chapter Five 26
Chapter Six 31
Chapter Seven 38
Chapter Eight 43
Chapter Nine 51
Chapter Ten 58
Chapter Eleven 63
Chapter Twelve 69
Chapter Thirteen 75
Chapter Fourteen 80

Chapter Fifteen	86
Chapter Sixteen	92
Chapter Seventeen	99
Chapter Eighteen	104
Chapter Nineteen	110
Chapter Twenty	115
Chapter Twenty-One	121
Chapter Twenty-Two	125
Chapter Twenty-Three	128
Chapter Twenty-Four	134
Chapter Twenty-Five	137
Chapter Twenty-Six	143
Chapter Twenty-Seven	148
Chapter Twenty-Eight	154
Chapter Twenty-Nine	161
Chapter Thirty	166
Chapter Thirty-One	171
Chapter Thirty-Two	175
Chapter Thirty-Three	182
Chapter Thirty-Four	186
Epilogue	191
A Favor, Please?	201
Books by Arianna Fraser	203
Free Books!	205
About The Author	207

PREFACE

Relentless - An Arranged Marriage Scottish Mafia Romance, is set in the brutal world of organized crime. These Scotsmen are not messing around.

As such, there is violence, detailed battle action, murder, kidnapping, explicit and delightfully detailed sex between consenting partners, and some troubling - though not hugely detailed - descriptions of human trafficking.

If these things are not to your taste, I thank you for stopping by, but please find something you might enjoy more.

Still here? Excellent! Grab a glass of wine or a bag of Cheetos and let's get started. As always, thank you for reading and supporting my stories.

~Fondly, Arianna

FORWARD

Dear friends,

If you've read Perilous - A Dark College Mafia Romance and its extended epilogue, I wanted to catch you up on the timing for Relentless - An Arranged Marriage Scottish Mafia Romance. This story is set shortly after the rescue mission Mala and Cormac went on in the extended epilogue. Relentless is about five years after Mala and Cormac met in Perilous.

If you've not read Perilous, it's not necessary to enjoy Relentless.

Happy Reading! Arianna

PROLOGUE

Cameron...

"What do you mean, you've gone in!"

"I'm sorry, we had to. They had a convoy of trucks coming in for the girls." Ferr, my second is shouting into his phone, I can hear glass shattering and gunfire in the background.

"Hamish, how close are we?" I ask my driver, low and urgent. I don't want Ferr to know how far away we are. We'd just landed at a private airfield outside of Moscow. His team was supposed to wait so we could storm the warehouse together.

"Boss, we're still thirty minutes away," he whispers, stepping on the gas. "At least."

"Ferr, you listen to me. You get the hell out of there. Mow those fuckers down but do not stay put, understood?"

"...Girls... still too close... hold off and..." The sound of bullets gets louder, drowning out his voice and then something worse.

The roar and rushing sound of flames. The screaming of my men.

Then, nothing.

CHAPTER ONE

In which this is the worst wedding ever.

Morana...

It's my wedding day.

And I am so screwed.

The hideous old troll waiting at the altar for me is close to sixty. He has red veins running through his nose and cheeks ruddy from decades of heavy drinking and a heavy, oily tobacco stink coming from his pores.

I'd discovered all of this when I met him last night for the first time, when he cornered me and kissed me. Bile rises in my throat and I take a couple of deep breaths. If I vomit down the front of my Monique Lhuillier wedding gown, my father will take his belt to me.

Not that my husband-to-be will be any better.

Vadik Stepanov is one of the Moscow Six, the Bratva families that rule the crime world. He's made most of his money in human trafficking, strip clubs, bordellos... he is the lowest form of life that profits from human suffering, he's next-level evil.

Anatoly Ivanov, my father, is giddy with joy over the match. My life will likely be horrific - and if I'm lucky, short - but his only interest is in the alliance my marriage will bring between the Stepanov Bratva and his.

Our family's organization under his father's rule was fearsome and powerful. The Ivanov Bratva no longer strikes terror in the hearts of men, and oh, how my father misses those days. Bad luck and dwindling connections have shrunk our reach. I could say that it is the *current* Pakhan's sloppy leadership and poor business decisions that have brought us so low, though that would mean a beating I may not come back from.

If I'd had the choice to plan anything about my wedding day, I would have loved to have been married in one of the exquisite little chapels at St. Basil's Cathedral near Red Square. It's some of the most brilliant, colorful architecture Russia has to offer. But of course, the spectacle both Bratvas insist on can only be contained in the massive Cathedral of Christ the Savior, the biggest Russian Orthodox church in Moscow.

"Turn your head, Miss."

The stylist is a stern German woman who's roughly brushing my hair into a complicated updo. I don't know where they got her from, but she looks more like a prison warden than a stylist. She had walked into the bride's dressing room at the Cathedral of Christ the Saviour and told me to remove my clothes.

I could see two Ivanov guards in the hallway, grinning at me. "I'll do it as soon as you shut the door," I said coldly.

Thank god, she didn't put up a fight about that, using her energy instead to wrestle me into a wedding dress that makes me look like a cake topper. It's a gigantic chiffon monstrosity lavishly encrusted with Swarovski crystals that sounds like a wind chime when I move.

Fortunately, I'm completely covered up by the time the door opens without a knock.

"Your father sent me in to make sure you were behaving and not crying like some spoiled little bitch."

"Artim Ivanov, my dear cousin," my reflection in the giant mirror shows I'm giving him a grin that looks like I want to take a chunk out of his face, which I do. Since he has no sons, Artim is my father's heir.

Artim is an evil fuck. Possibly, worse than my father. "If anyone knows how to cry like a spoiled little bitch, it would be you."

His hand comes up and my German warden steps in front of me. "No bruises for the ceremony!" she barks.

"You should watch your tongue, Morana Ivanova, you may be marrying into the Stepanov Bratva, but we are still family." He leans closer and I force myself not to shrink away. "The old fuck you're about to marry isn't going to live much longer."

"I'll be sure to mention to my new husband that you're looking forward to his death, Artim Ivanov."

My cousin should be furious, trying to hit me again but instead, he leans back against the little antique couch. "You won't have time for that tonight, my cousin," Artim says happily. "You're not aware of the Stepanov wedding night traditions, are you?" So happily. He is never this happy unless it involves a bottle of vodka and a couple of terrified strippers.

"The Stepanov men believe in showing their bride how things will be right away," he says, leaning closer. I can see the madness dancing in his eyes. "They beat the shit out of their brides and then fuck them in front of their men, just to show the women who's in charge. When he does that to you tonight, cousin, he's showing his Bratva that you are lower than all of them."

He could be lying. It would be just like Artim to do that to me. But remembering the flabby, heavy body of my "fiancé" pressed against me last night when he forced me to kiss him, I know he's telling the truth. It was disgusting, like a horse licking ice cream.

The desire to throw up down the front of my wedding dress is stronger than ever.

"Thank you for the encouraging little speech, Artim Ivanov." I smile sweetly. "Now, why don't you get the fuck out of here?"

His hands curl into fists, and I can feel his need to hurt me. I don't know if it's my stern prison warden slash hairdresser or the knowledge that something much worse is going to happen to me tonight, but he grins and leaves the room.

There will be no beloved family faces smiling at me, only guards to make sure I can't escape. If my horrible cousin is right, tonight is about to be the worst one of my miserable existence.

But I can't run. I tried that already. Once.

There's a loud knock on the door and the stylist and I both jump a little, she burns the tip of my ear with the curling iron.

"What is it?" she shouts.

"The Pakhan wishes for his bride to wear a necklace from the Stepanov family collection." The messenger's boredom could not be any more obvious, even behind the closed door.

My warden opens the door and a Ruger is pressed against her forehead, pushing her back in.

"Ah, ah!" The gunman warns, "Don't reach for that gun you have strapped to your ankle. Sit the fuck down."

It's as if pieces of reality broke apart and reassembled in some form that I don't understand. There's an alarmingly large man in a tux holding a gun on her as another man whose entire being screams "bodyguard" quickly locks the door and then zip-ties her to a chair and stuffs a gag in her mouth, taping it closed. Her eyes are bulging in fury and there's a lot of muffled screaming happening.

The man rolls his eyes, his Russian accent disappearing as he speaks in English. "Knock her out."

Her face goes beet red as the bodyguard quickly plunges a needle into her neck.

Turning to look at me, the man doesn't lower his gun, but he holds up another hypodermic needle. "I can shove this into your neck and drag your useless body out the window. I can't guarantee I won't drop you a couple of times if I have to do that. If you're bright enough to remember that I'm holding a gun and do what I tell you, I won't knock you out."

This dress is too tight. I can't breathe. "What is- where are the guards- what-"

He grabs me by the throat and lifts the needle.

Maybe it's because I'm terrified of being unconscious and helpless to stop whatever could happen to me. Maybe it's because this giant in a tux is... offering me a choice? I shove against his chest.

"I won't fight! Just don't drug me."

He leans closer. "If you scream or try to run away, I will put this needle through your eye, do you understand?" If his voice was a touch, I'd have frostbite, but I can feel the hate and fury simmering behind his words.

"You're quite clear," I hiss, moving reluctantly toward the window as he gives me a little shove. His man already has it open, struggling a bit with the stubborn old wooden frame.

Looking out, I flinch. "We're two stories up!"

He slides out the window, hangs on the side for a moment, then lands gracefully on the balls of his feet. In dress shoes. Before I can make a run for the door, his bodyguard scoops me up and throws me out the window. The voluminous skirt of my dress hooks on something and slows my fall, and the giant catches me easily.

"Cut her loose," he calls up softly, and the other man slices through the material before leaping down and landing almost silently.

He had to put that syringe away to jump, right? I'll kick off my shoes and take off the second he puts me down...

Except, he doesn't. The giant bastard throws me over his

shoulder and races toward the service entrance. I'm bouncing on his broad shoulder and each time I land against him, it knocks the breath out of me. My hair's falling out of the fancy updo and into my eyes, I push it back long enough to see one of my father's men standing at the open window, shouting.

"How did they break through that bolted door so fast?" the giant grumbles.

"Aye, I locked it and shoved the couch in front of it," his guard says sourly.

There's a florist van in front of us and yet another dark-suited man whips open the back door. I yelp when the giant throws me in, where I land on a box of lilies. I manage to sit up just long enough to get knocked over again as the van takes off.

Staring up at the roof as the smell of crushed flowers nearly chokes me, I'm horrified to feel a laugh bubbling up. Stolen from my wedding to a monster, by a monstrously huge man who threatened to jam a needle in my eye.

The legendary bad luck of the Ivanov's continues.

CHAPTER TWO

In which this kidnapping is not going smoothly.

Cameron...

Checking my watch, I see that we're on time. Two minutes ahead, in fact. "The jet's fueled and ready?"

"Aye, already on the runway," Hamish says. Studying his serious expression, I nod to myself. He's a good man, hard-working. He's not Ferr, but he'll make an excellent second.

The image of Ferr's broken, bloody body assaults me and my jaw tightens.

"Zip-tie the lass," I call over my shoulder to Grant. I hear a low grunt and some cursing.

"Stop fightin' me! Ya' ain't going anywhere-"

"I came with you *ublyudki,* you bastards! You don't have to tie me up. The giant up there said-"

With a sigh, I release my seatbelt and slide into the back. "Do you want me to bring out that needle?"

Her long, blonde hair is all over her face and she glares at me between the curls. "No! I've done what you asked, I didn't fight! Don't let this ape tie me up."

Even in her torn wedding gown, stained with dirt and flower pollen, she's a sight. Her furious eyes are the shade of the violets in my mother's greenhouse, and her pretty pink mouth is twisted into a snarl.

"Don't you honor your agreements, kidnapper?" she spat.

Breaking into laughter, I grab her wrists, holding her still as he zip-ties them together. She's still kicking furiously and one of her high heels catches Grant in the shoulder.

"Those feckin' death shoes of hers just drew blood," he scowls, irritably examining the cut as he yanks them off her feet.

"Did the wee girl hurt you, big guy?" I laugh, "Finish the job."

The van makes a sudden, violent swerve to the left and I hear angry horns around out. "Tire's out, Boss!"

"And thank ye' for that unnecessary update," I grumbled, pulling my gun and returning to the passenger seat. "They could not have caught up with us."

"No," Hamish said, checking the road behind us. "It's just a flat. How fecking stupid is that?"

"How close is our backup?"

He listened to his earpiece. "Three minutes, tops."

"Tell 'em to *greas ort,* hurry the feck up! A flat tire? How the hell does that happen?" I snap, looking over my shoulder to see that Grant has finally subdued the woman, even though she's still writhing like an enraged eel. Putting my earpiece back in, I hear the increasingly agitated discussion.

"Aerial surveillance shows we've got men in pursuit," the other driver says.

Checking my watch, I growl. We're now two and a half minutes behind schedule. My missions are never behind. There are six different roads around that church. There's no way they could have put together enough teams to track us that fast.

A black SUV pulls up behind us and I have the girl out of the back of the van and on my lap in the new car in seconds. Now, we're seven and a half minutes behind schedule.

As we race toward the airfield, I listen to the chatter between our crew conducting aerial surveillance and the pilot, who is already starting up the engines.

"Two minutes, Boss," Hamish assures me as we stop for a red light.

"Sir, it looks like there are three vehicles in pursuit. They must be anticipating we'd use this airfield." Colin's our drone expert and sounds genuinely apologetic that the threat is increasing.

The light changes to green and the car in front of us lurches and then sputters to a stop.

"Are you feckin' kidding me?" I shout, unfortunately right in the girl's ear and she jumps, the back of her head knocking painfully into my nose, which gleefully starts spurting blood.

Hamish deftly gets around the stalled car, barely avoiding an oncoming tanker truck and we take the turn onto the airfield on two tires. We race past two other jets, their crews' startled faces following our progress. Throwing the girl over my shoulder, I lope up the jet stairs and the flight attendant slams the door shut as my last man enters.

Checking my watch. Eight minutes and twenty seconds behind schedule. This shite *never* happens.

I'm strapping my still-bound captive into her seat when she raises her bound hands to point at my face.

"Your nose is bleeding down your fancy tuxedo, *kidnapper*."

CHAPTER THREE

In which we meet Miss Kevin and a charcuterie board.

Morana...

"Welcome abroad, Miss Ivanova, may I get you something to drink?"

My kidnapper had retreated to the bathroom after the jet took off to stop the blood streaming from his nose. I'd hit it pretty hard but in my defense, he shouted in my ear. Pity I didn't break it.

"Miss Ivanova?" The flight attendant is still hovering over me, his smile a bit frayed around the edges.

"Yes," I hold up my zip-tied wrists. "Could you get these off for me? Being tied up like a farm animal makes it a little hard to take a drink."

"I'm terribly sorry," he did look apologetic, "but I am unable to accommodate that request. But I could get you a drink with a straw?"

"Do you see a lot of kidnap victims and that's why you're such a warm and helpful host?" I ask, "Because this kind of solicitous behavior is over the top."

He smiles helplessly. "Well, my name is Ian, let me know if I can get you anything." Ian is a nice-looking person, sandy blonde hair and a slender build, and he has that eager puppy expression as if my not letting him get me a drink is causing him real pain.

This jet is gorgeous and could easily seat fifty people, though it looks like my kidnapper brought a smaller crew, maybe around ten, or eleven men. There's a huge main area with groupings of luxurious leather seating, a bar against one wall, and what looks like a conference room in the next area of the jet.

I don't know if it's good or bad that the man who stole me from my wedding is wielding such an impressive level of wealth, maybe as much as the Stepanov Bratva. That will be helpful, though, when my hideous groom comes after him to kill everyone he loves.

There could be no greater insult than what this man has done.

I'm left alone, his men gathered in other seating areas, playing cards and laughing. They carefully avoided looking at me at all, as if they'd been forbidden to. The giant who'd dragged me out of the church is pacing in the conference room, speaking on the phone. Based on his sharp steps and how he's dragging his hand through his dark brown hair, he's not happy.

The man is gorgeous. I can admit it even while I'm scared and furious at the same time. He's widely muscled to fill out his tall frame, his biceps are bigger than my head, and his green eyes are nearly glowing under those stern, dark brows. There are tattoos on his wrists, like tally marks. Is he keeping track of how many people he's killed with his huge claw hands?

His stern gaze darts to me and I narrow my eyes in return. Putting away his phone, he strides through the cabin and seats himself across from me.

"You've pissed off both the Stepanov and the Ivanov Bratvas," I comment, "I hope it was worth it."

"Your Pakhan has a lot to pay for," he says coldly, "and it starts with you."

Torn between begging him to let me go or bravado, I choose bravado. "It's your funeral," I shrug. "Ian, your pleasant flight attendant looks like he's going to cry every time he offers me a beverage. Since the chances of me escaping from this jet mid-flight are about as good as being hit by a meteor, could you take these off me?"

One of his dark brows rises, as if he's shocked that I'm not cowering and pleading for my life. Pulling a stiletto out of his boot, he slices through the ties on my wrists and ankles. Rubbing my wrists I continue to glare at him as he looks me over more thoroughly.

"Ya' look like a Disney princess exploded all over ya'."

"This dress wasn't my choice," I say grimly. "What's your name, anyway? You're not wearing a mask or keeping a bag over my head, so you obviously don't care if I know who you are."

Ian puts a glass filled with amber liquid down in front of him, and he takes a long drink before he answers me, just to be a dick about it. "Cameron MacTavish."

"Why did you kidnap me from my wedding, Cameron MacTavish?"

He crossed his legs, doing that manly thing where they rest their ankle on the other knee. "I told you. You are the first step."

"The first step in what?"

"Burning your father's Bratva to ash. And given all the sick shite your intended is into, I'm thinking I might finish him off, too."

It feels like a cold fist is squeezing my heart. "I see. And what role do I play in this?"

Cameron leaned forward, his handsome features like stone. "Be quiet, don't cause any trouble. If you do try to get away, and maybe ask someone for help? I'll kill them."

He gets up and joins one of the other groups, leaving me alone.

Even if Cameron's man Hamish hadn't happily announced in his searing Scottish accent, "It's good to be home, lads!" I would have known we were landing in Edinburgh.

I remember the first time I visited here, the incredible contrast of vivid green and rough-hewn rock. I'd managed to escape for a couple of precious hours while my father was conducting business. I watched a gathering of bagpipe players in their colorful tartans and how the music soared over the slate roofs of the city, into the cloudy sky and my heart filled to bursting.

It was precious to me, even if it only lasted an hour.

Glumly gathering up handfuls of tattered chiffon to avoid tripping down the jet stairs, I wonder if Cameron would let me change out of this thing. He doesn't look my way as I'm put into one black Range Rover and he gets in the passenger seat of another one.

If I just reached out... I could crack something over the driver's head. The car would veer off the road. I'd be out of here and racing away to... Nowhere. I'm in a ridiculous, tattered wedding dress and I'm barefoot. The other guard would catch up with me in a heartbeat.

Cameron's threat about killing anyone I asked for help; did he mean it? I think he would. Just because he's Scottish and not Russian, did I really think he would be merciful?

We've been driving for half an hour or so when the Range Rover turns onto a private lane, the iron gate closing behind us with an ominous clanging sound. I'm not familiar with this part of Edinburgh, it is close to the river, though, and the huge stone house in front of us is beautiful, a Georgian style with lush trees and towering urns of flowers.

Essentially, the last place I'd expect someone like Cameron to live.

Of course, what do I know about my kidnapper? Maybe he lives here with his beautiful wife and five kids and I'll be put in the basement in a cell. The front door opens and an elegant woman in a formal suit and tie nods at me, smiling warmly.

"Miss Ivanova, welcome. Please come in and let me make you more comfortable."

It's hard to trust a smile from anyone associated with the man who kidnapped me, but I manufacture a weak one in return. "Thank you."

She leads me down a long hallway, colorful old oriental rugs softening the marble floor. Since I'm shoeless, my feet appreciate it. Instead of taking me down into a sinister basement, she opens a tall door and I walk into a two-story library. My family's mansion has a library like this, but I was never allowed in it, and though I would sneak books out to read when my father wasn't around, I doubt most of those rows upon rows of beautiful leather-bound books were ever opened.

This library, however, looks more lived-in. There's a blaze going in the huge fireplace, framed photos of who I'm assuming are family and friends on the walls, and a book left open on the armrest of one of the big leather chairs.

"Please, Miss Ivanova, have a seat. I have some refreshments coming for you." The woman has short, silver hair and wears that butler's suit like a boss.

Seating myself uneasily on the sofa, I ask, "What should I call you?"

"Miss Kevin," she says pleasantly.

"A pleasure to meet you, Miss Kevin." Another woman hurries in with a tray, putting it on the table in front of me. There is a nice array of cured meats and cheeses, along with some thinly sliced fruit and crackers.

"Can I pour you a glass?" Miss Kevin holds up a bottle of wine, "It's a lovely Pinot Noir."

Every part of me wants to grab that wine right from her hand and guzzle it straight from the bottle, but this seems like a bad time to be even the slightest bit impaired. "No thank you, but a bottle of water would be wonderful."

"Of course," she says, smiling pleasantly, pulling one from the wine fridge underneath the bar. "I'll give you a moment alone, but just call for me if you need anything."

"Thank you," I say faintly.

This is so surreal. I'm sitting in a proper old library with a butler named Miss Kevin and a charcuterie board.

By the time the door opens again, my feet are propped up on the coffee table and I've made substantial inroads into the snacks. My father put me on a fast three days ago because the dressmaker said I'd gained weight and couldn't fit into my wedding dress. She was lying, she just hated me for... I don't know, being me, I guess. She'd stuck pins into my skin while pretending to fit me for the dress until I told her the next one was going through her nose to use as an impromptu piercing.

"Made yourself at home, I see." Cameron is looking at me like I'm a mess his puppy left behind.

"There's still some of those chocolate-covered almonds if you want," I shrug.

"I'm fine." He checks his watch, a nice stainless steel Patek Philippe. "Why don't you go get cleaned up?"

I huff out a furious little laugh. "Getting dropped out of a window and thrown into a van doesn't help a girl look her best. *So* sorry."

Ignoring me, he steps out into the hallway. "There's a bathroom to the right. You have ten minutes."

"Ten minutes for what?" He didn't answer me, shutting the library door behind him.

When I came back, I'd managed to brush the worst of the snarls and the crushed flower petals out of my hair and washed my face

17

and hands. Most of my fancy bride makeup had already smeared off my face at some point.

He isn't alone, there's another man with him, graying hair and a look of faint disapproval, and he has a priest's collar.

"Morana." It's the first time Cameron has used my name. "This is Father Barclay. He's here to marry us."

CHAPTER FOUR

In which we were incorrect. THIS is the worst wedding ever.

Cameron...

I watch with a certain amount of satisfaction as the blood drains from the Ivanova girl's face, leaving her sheet white.

"What?" she wheezes, swaying a little.

"Father Barclay is my family's priest," I say patiently, "he's here to marry us."

She's looking between him and me, taking deep, heaving breaths and it's doing some nice things for her breasts, swelling enticingly over the top of that ridiculous gown.

"If he's your family's priest, then you can't kill him if I ask for help."

Damn the girl.

"Father, this man kidnapped me! I don't want to be here!" Morana's eyes are wide, trying to appeal to him, her tone sweet and desperate, like I'm about to throw her into an alligator pit. "Please, help me get out of here. He kidnapped me from my wedding!"

With a sigh, Father Barclay folds his hands in front of him. "My child, did you truly wish to marry Vadik Stepanov?"

She wasn't expecting that.

"I beg your pardon?"

Gently taking her elbow, he guided her to the sofa, sitting across from her. "I know something of your story. Vadik Stepanov is a curse against mankind. He steals and sells souls into slavery all over the world. Do you wish to be married to him?"

Her pretty pink mouth is trying to form words, and it's oddly titillating. "Well- no, of course not! I know he's a monster. But if I don't…" Morana shudders, a full-body tremble that seems involuntary. "My father. Well… he'll…"

"Aye, I've heard of your father, too," he says grimly. "While I canna' say that Cameron has made this the best of beginnings," he narrows his eyes at me, "his intentions are sincere. If you marry him, your safety is guaranteed."

"Vadik Stepanov will never forgive this insult," she says wearily. "You don't understand what you've set off here. He will come after you with everything he's got. This puts your family in danger, too. The MacTavish Mafia. Yes," she nodded at my raised brow, "I figured out the significance of your last name. You're powerful. Your family has connections in Russia. But not with my father's Bratva. Why are you doing this?"

"That's not your concern," I say coldly. "You have a choice. Marry me and enjoy the security of my family name, or I'll just keep you as a whore."

"My son! That is not acceptable!" Father Barclay's voice is like thunder.

"Forgive me, Father. But this is between Miss Ivanova and me. Lass, make your choice."

I've already noticed that when she's angry, her eyes turn a deeper shade of violet, more like thunderstorm clouds. "It guarantees nothing. When he comes, Vadik will torture and kill me, too." Giving a short, bitter laugh, she stood up. "But why not? I'm dressed for the occasion, after all."

Morana's expression changes, it's not just rage. Malice and something I can't fully interpret take over.

Still, I nod. "Good girl."

The ceremony is quick, Father Barclay is not pleased with me, but the argument that she's safer with me won him over. Without her heels, Morana barely reaches my shoulder, I can still smell the scent of crushed lilies and roses in her hair.

"...you may kiss the bride."

Looking down at her beautiful, wary face, all I can remember is the sight of Ferr's broken, bloody body. The screams from his mother and sisters when I went to tell them the news.

Taking her jaw between my fingers and thumb, I kiss her harshly, feeling her stiffen. But damn it all, her lips are pillowy soft and sweet, and suddenly, I want to take her lower one and bite it, thrust my tongue in her mouth, and play with hers… My hand slides around to the back of her neck to hold her in place while I push her lips apart with my tongue, pressing harder. A little noise escapes her throat and I pull back abruptly. She looks just as shocked as I feel.

Walking Father Barclay to the door is a chilly experience. "Thank you for your blessing, Father." I pull a thick envelope out of my jacket. "A small contribution to the parish."

He is not impressed.

"I am disappointed in you, my son," he says coldly. "Giving God's blessing to this union was… complicated."

"You have saved her from a far worse fate than me, Father," I sigh. It doesn't matter what I say. The man is planted firmly in the doorway.

"The parish ladies have been raising money for a new roof and organ for the church," he says, eyeing me keenly.

"I believe there is enough in that envelope for one or the other, Father."

He shrugs under his cassock. "One… or the other. A problem, you see. If we purchase the organ and the roof leaks and destroys it, it would be a tragedy. Should we repair the roof but there is no music to lift the spirit, well…"

There's no getting out of this, and I'm going to punish Morana for kicking up such a fuss about marrying me. Father Barclay is clear that he wants both the roof and the organ to assuage his conscience. I've known this man since birth and I don't believe he has a conscience, but… "I understand. I will have a matching sum delivered to you tomorrow."

"Go with God, son." He smiles serenely.

My new bride is standing exactly where I left her in the library, the glass of champagne Miss Kevin insisted on pouring for her still clutched in her hand after we'd signed the marriage license.

"What the hell just happened?" Morana blurts.

Taking her left hand, I hold it up to eye level, the enormous diamond ring on her finger glittering in the firelight. "We got married. You are legally mine."

"Legally?" She shakes her head. "That- he wasn't a real priest, was he? This is some sick joke that's part of your genuinely insane master plan."

Bypassing the flute of Dom Perignon left for me, I pour three fingers of O'Rourke, drinking it faster than a good whiskey deserves. "It is part of my master plan, but no. Not a joke. It's real." I smile at her malevolently, enjoying her fury. "We were bound before God and it is completely legal. Iron-clad, in fact. It was quite expensive, thanks to your dramatic flair with the kidnapping speech, but we are married."

"I have to get out of this dress." She's pulling at the lace and chiffon at the neckline, breathing hard. "This is choking me, I have to get it off me-"

"Hey now, hey lass, you're having a panic attack."

Morana is pale and shaking, still pulling at the material and I quickly seat her on my lap. "Tell me three things you can see."

Her panicked gasps are turning to wheezing and I yank apart the back of the gown. "I can't…"

"Aye, you can, tell me three things."

"The… the desk," she rasps, "your drink. The window."

"Good girl, such a good lass," I murmur, "now, two things you can hear." Rubbing her back, I avoid looking at her heaving breasts. God, I'm a sick fuck.

"*Ogon' v kamine-* I mean, the fire in the fireplace. The- the wind outside."

Her breathing's better now, almost normal, and some color's back in her cheeks. After we sit quietly for a moment, I lift my glass. "Here, lass. Take a drink. You need it more than I do." I offer her my whiskey.

She makes a face after swallowing it. "That's horrible."

Laughing, I raise my glass again. "This is from an O'Rourke cask aged for twenty-five years. Would you like another sip?"

"No, thank you." Rubbing her eyes, she says, "How did you know what to do? When…"

"Your panic attack? My little sister used to get 'em a lot. We all learned how to talk her down."

My little sister Sorcha, who was kidnapped by the Triad fucks who work with Morana's former fiance. Just another reason to burn his Bratva to ash.

Morana must have felt me stiffen because her spine straightened again. "I'm sorry. About your sister, I mean. I hope she's doing better."

Most days… I think.

"Aye, she's fine. You need a bath, proper clothes, and sleep. We'll talk in the morning."

She looked at me with a little furrow between her brows. "You're not going to try to do… that?"

"Don't take this personally, lass, but you're not at your most enticing right now, so no. I don't want to do *that*. Miss Kevin will take you upstairs and get you settled."

As if she'd been hovering outside the door, Miss Kevin walks in with her usual gracious smile in place. "Mrs. MacTavish, if you'll come with me?"

It clearly takes my blushing bride a moment to realize that Miss Kevin is addressing her, but she quickly gets off my lap, holding the dress in place as it slips down. She looks back at me again, still puzzled.

"We'll talk in the morning," I nod toward the door where my butler is waiting. Without another word, Morana hurries out of the room.

"How did it go?"

"Smooth as silk," I lie, "as always."

"Hmm…" My elder brother Cormac has been the head of the MacTavish clan for five years now and has adopted a certain gravitas that I find deeply annoying. "What do you think of the girl?"

"Morana? She's got a sassy mouth on her, but she handled the kidnapping like a professional."

He snorts, "It's probably not her first one, though I can't picture that tight-fisted bastard putting out any money to ransom her back."

"She was the only asset Ivanov had left," I say, "he must be shitting himself right now."

"Aye," Cormac agrees. He hesitates for a moment. "I just received another piece of information from Nikandr in Moscow. Be careful with this girl."

"What do ya' mean?" I frown. Be careful of Morana? She's a little thing. Picturing her wheezing through the panic attack on my lap made me feel warmer toward her than I should. But she was soft, and light against me. My bride smells like crushed lilies and roses, with a slight, wintery scent, like frost and peppermint.

"Our people weren't sure how much she knew about Bratva business. But Nikandr spotted her at one of the auctions last week, all dressed up. Drinkin' and laughin' while girls were crying, getting sold off."

Disgust curdles in my stomach. I certainly didn't marry the woman for love, but I assumed she was another victim in her family's fucked-up plans. She was *there*. She'd seen what the alliance between her family and Stepanov was creating.

CHAPTER FIVE

In which Morana fights back with all the tools at her disposal: her profound Karmic misfortune.

Morana...

Waking up the next morning to a gentle tap on the door, I take a moment to appreciate the quiet. No screaming, no slamming doors, no aggressive trail of cigar smoke as my father storms up and down the halls...

"Good morning, Mrs. MacTavish, I have breakfast for you." It's Miss Kevin, with her gentle smile and a full tray of food.

"Please don't call me that," I blurt.

A small wrinkle appears on her flawless forehead. "What would you prefer?"

"Just Morana, please?"

That tiny wrinkle appears again. "I fear that would be too informal. I would not be comfortable addressing the lady of the house in such a way." She brightens. "Madame Morana? Mistress Morana?"

"Not the second one, please," I say, "it sounds like a character in a BDSM romance."

The first one sounds like I'm running a brothel, I think, *but I guess it could be worse.*

Back home in Moscow, when anyone was actually required to speak to me directly, it was as Miss Morana, but I guess we're held to a higher standard here.

"Very well," she says, equanimity returned. "Madame Morana, would you prefer to eat first or shall I draw you a bath?"

"I…" The Ivanovs may have fallen from the heights of power that our Bratva once enjoyed, but I grew up around wealth. However, having someone 'draw me a bath' is a bit much. "Maybe you could just sit with me for a minute while I eat? Tell me more about this place?"

Miss Kevin doesn't sit, but she folds her hands in front of her and smiles at me approvingly. "I shall be happy to tell you about the manor. It was built in 1858, a Georgian style that was-"

"No, I mean, who lives here? Is your boss pure evil? Is he good to the people he employs?"

"Oh. Well, yes. Master Cameron is an excellent employer. He is firm, but fair."

I barely avoid rolling my eyes.

"He is very loyal and generous to those who are loyal to him," she continues.

"Uh, huh."

Apparently, I'm not enthusiastic enough because she smiles reassuringly. "You need not worry about your safety, of course. There is always a rotating unit of guards on site, in and out of the house. Security here is unparalleled."

"Sort of like Downton Abbey, but with firearms?" I ask.

A rise of one eyebrow tells me my levity is unwelcome.

There's a giant crash outside my window and we hurry over to look. The wind has been roaring around the house all night. One of the oak trees lining the driveway has landed right on top of an expensive sports car - a Bugatti, I think - and it's crushed beyond repair. Three of the guards are surrounding the car with equal expressions of alarm as Cameron is yelling, pacing around the car with his hands on his hips.

"Goodness, this is a terrible thing," she says, "that is Mr. MacTavish's favorite car."

"He was supposed to talk to me this morning," I mumbled.

"Oh," Miss Kevin said apologetically, "I was instructed to tell you that he had some issues in London that required his immediate attention."

Really...

Folding my arms as I watch his angry gesticulation, I know two things. Cameron MacTavish is a dismissive asshole as well as a kidnapper, and also, that the Ivanov streak of bad luck and utter misfortune continues.

I turn so Miss Kevin doesn't see my grin.

Good.

Spending the next three days wandering around Cameron's absurdly large house, I do a lot of smiling and nodding, like this is all fine and I'm happy playing Lady of the Manor while that *svoloch'*, that bastard of a husband is off conducting meetings, or murders, whatever it is Scottish criminals do.

He's called Miss Kevin - I overheard the conversation - but never spoke to me. Does he expect me to just... what? Sit here and marinate in his attractively decorated Scottish prison? Because as pretty as this place is, as kind as Miss Kevin is to me, it's definitely a prison. There's a guard who stands outside my bedroom door - and he scared the living hell out of me the first morning when I left the room - and there's no leaving a single room in this place without one of his dark-suited minions following me.

"I'm going to the bathroom," I tell the guard currently breathing down my neck. "I'm going to soak a towel in toilet water. If you're hovering here like a *sliznyak,* a creep when I come out,

I'm going to wrap it around your head and smother you. Do you understand me?"

He steps back. Just one step.

Kidnapped from my wedding to a monster, married to a psychopath who just dumps me and runs off, and... I slump sadly on the toilet. That first night, when he put me on his lap and comforted me, he smelled so nice, the solid feel of his thick thighs and chest. It felt... like maybe this wasn't the worst thing that could happen to me. It was nothing, I was nothing. Just a pawn that-

I jump half a foot as someone pounds on the door.

"That *Sukin syn,* that son of a bitch!"

As I leap up, I stumble against the wrought iron towel holder, which comes loose and slams into the base of the porcelain throne I'd just vacated. It cracks into three pieces and I shriek as I slip in the water, heading toward the door. It slams open and I slide into the man standing there, knocking him over and both of us into the hallway, instantly soaked in the toilet deluge.

Looking down, I see Cameron under me, glaring. "I see you've been settling in."

Indignantly, I struggle free of him. Gracefully leaping to his feet, he grabs my hand and hauls me up like a sack of flour. "Thanks, I guess," I snap. "Also, *poshel ty,* screw you."

I'm covered in toilet water and he's in a gorgeously expensive suit, looking like sex, and sin, and pain.

"Excuse me?" Cameron's voice is low and dangerous, and looking around us, I realize we have company. There's another extremely tall man with dark hair and eyes, wearing a huge grin and a nice suit. He must be a brother.

"I like her," he says to Cameron. "She's got this insane energy about her, like a scorpion in a toaster."

"Dougal, my... wife, Morana Ivanova MacTavish," Cameron says, looking like introducing me is about as appealing as having his face smashed in with a brick. "This is my younger brother, Dougal MacTavish."

"I'm the more handsome one, as you can see," Dougal says, offering his hand.

Looking down at my wet clothes, I shake my head. "I'm sorry, but they'd have to douse you in petrol to get the germs off you. Nice to meet you, I'll just be… going away now."

Hurrying up the stairs, utterly mortified and equally enraged, I hear him cheerfully say, "At least she flushed the loo first."

CHAPTER SIX

In which Morana gains her vengeance via soup.

Cameron...

"You really left a bride as fine as Morana to do business in London?" Dougal laughs at me. "Jaysus, Mary, and Joseph, you're an eejit."

"It's not that simple, you arsehole," I snap, rubbing my eyes. I'd kept my mind off Morana by working every waking second while I was in London, and I'm fecking exhausted. "I'm not sure what to do with her."

"Well, you put children in her. You know how that works, right?"

"Thanks, brother. The coach showed us a film in health class twenty years ago, I'm sure I can remember the key points," I snarl.

"Then what's the problem?" Dougal helps himself to my scotch. "The girl has to know she traded the hell up by getting you instead of that nasty old feck."

"I did my research on her, obviously," I say, "she seemed like your standard Bratva princess, trapped by her arsehole da'. Mom died in childbirth with her. Da' blamed her and sent her off to boarding school when she was only five. Excellent grades and halfway through a degree in Art History from the Royal Danish Academy when Ivanov pulled her out to marry Stepanov."

"It's all making ya' look better and better," he agrees, finishing his drink. "Why aren't you upstairs right now, naked and makin' her call out for a higher power?"

"It's complicated."

"It's complicated?" Dougal scoffs, "Who are you, a fifteen-year-old girl setting up your relationship profile on Facebook?"

"I talked with Cormac the night I took her," I say. "One of our people in the Ivanov Bratva told him that she knows exactly what Stepanov and her arsehole da' are into. He said he spotted her at one of the slave auctions, all dressed up, drinking and laughing."

He makes a face as if someone just took a dump in his lap. "That's disgusting. Is the source certain? It doesn't seem likely a Bratva princess would be partying at a slave auction unless she was up next on the block."

I shrug. It is unusual, but I've learned in this business that women can be just as evil as men.

"Who was the source?" Dougal persists.

"Nikandr. He runs low-level security for the Ivanovs."

Tapping his fingers on the table, he shakes his head. "I'd get corroboration, brother. If she's evil enough to enjoy a sight such as that, she can't stay in the family."

"I'm aware, and I'm holding her here until we finish these bastards off. After that... Well, Father Barclay might make sure I'm excommunicated, but I'm not staying tied to a trafficker."

"If you haven't slept with her yet, you can always get an annulment," Dougal grins insolently. "Still, if you've not come up with any other information showing she's into the family business, give her the benefit of the doubt while you get some corroboration. That's a mighty serious accusation."

"Aye," I groan, "I'll just add that to the six missions Cormac, our mighty Chieftain wants me to handle, along with the acquisition of the two island properties and-"

"Let me call in a favor with the Turgenev Bratva," he suggests, "they've got an excellent spy network. Extra intelligence can't hurt."

"Just don't ask for too much," I caution, "we may still need their help with the Stepanov Bratva after I finish off the Ivanovs."

Cracking his knuckles, Dougal rises. "I'll get to work. It's hard to believe a lass that fine could watch an auction without setting the bar on fire." He instantly looks regretful. "Sorry, brother."

"No need," I say, cutting the discussion short.

Morana...

There's a knock on the door while I'm drying off from my second shower. If I hadn't flushed that toilet before Cameron had to pound on the door like a Neanderthal, I would be taking my third.

Still, the utter ignominy of lying there in the hall on top of the man was just... even for my consistent record of misfortune, that was so much extra.

"Madame Morana?" Miss Kevin inquires politely from behind the bathroom door. "Master Cameron would like you to join him for dinner in twenty minutes. Do you require any assistance in dressing?"

The image of being one of those useless ladies from the 1800s who would simply lie there as their servants dressed them rises up and I have to stifle a giggle. "No thank you, Miss Kevin. I'll be fine."

"Very well, I'll just leave some dress selections on your bed."

The dresses she's left out are all formal and seem a bit much for dinner, but maybe it's all black tie when the Laird of the Manor is home. Cameron MacTavish had been alarmingly thorough in his preparation for kidnapping me.

I had opened the door to what I thought was a closet that first morning to find a full dressing room, with rows upon rows of dresses and formal wear, athletic and leisure clothes, purses and shoes and boots. It appeared that he planned on keeping me for a while. There was also lingerie. Lots of lacy, silky bits in every color and the implication of it all had me bracing for a full-on assault from my imposed husband.

Until he disappeared hours after forcing me to marry him.

At least my prison was pretty. The room was decorated in a warm, feminine style with elegantly flowered linens and lots of comfortable pillows. The windows faced south, and I took advantage of all the weak sunlight the skies over Edinburgh could offer, reading on the big, built-in window bench and walking through the garden. Pretty or not, I missed University, and the few friends I'd made in Denmark. I hated not having a purpose, just drifting around this huge house with nothing useful to do.

After eyeing the dresses for a moment, I pick a black sleeveless one with a decent hemline that doesn't seem to make any kind of a statement. My ever-present guard is missing from my bedroom door, and I'm wondering if having Cameron home loosens the reins a little.

From the first time Miss Kevin attempted to serve me dinner in the formal dining room, at the foot of a table that could hold twenty people, I'd flatly refused. It was ridiculous. She wouldn't let me eat with the staff in the kitchen, calling it "unseemly," so we settled on meals on a tray in the library or my bedroom. Walking into the room, I see it's lavishly set with a huge bouquet of flowers and place settings at the head and foot of the table.

"Really," I chuckle to myself. "We're going to eat shouting at each other from fifteen feet away?"

Miss Kevin, who's uncorking a bottle of wine, looks at me apologetically. "Master Cameron wished to continue formal dining service."

"Meaning, he wants me on the other side of the room?" I ask

incredulously. She hums in a noncommittal fashion and I make my way to the bottom of the table, angrily seating myself.

Cameron's voice carries into the room to announce his arrival. "Have him send me the figures by tomorrow morning."

He strides in, dressed in a fresh suit - which makes my spiteful side grin - barking orders into the phone. Ugh. He's one of *those*. The men who sound like they're the general, roaring orders to the entire Roman Legion every time they pick up their cell. He finishes the call and seats himself, ignoring me.

"I believe you invited me to dinner?" I say a bit more caustically than I'd intended.

He looks up with a scowl as if noticing for the first time that I'm in the room. But the Laird of the Manor doesn't realize I endured a childhood of being treated as if I was not worthy of notice. This little show is nothing.

So, I raise one brow in polite inquiry and stare him down. "Oh, is this the talk you told me that we'd have 'tomorrow morning?' When was that? Last week?"

Cameron stares at me, unamused as Miss Kevin presents our elaborately prepared salads. When she makes her speedy exit, he growls, "I had other matters to attend to."

"Like the Bugatti?" I inquire solicitously, "That was a total loss, yes? A terrible shame."

Even narrowed threateningly, his eyes are a vivid green, dark, like the forest. "Family business. You will likely not see much of me; I'm kept very busy."

Well, that feel like a punch to my chest.

"Can you tell me anything?" I ask, "How long do I have to stay here?"

He frowns, "Did you forget the bit where I married ye'?"

"Please," I scoff, "this is a beautifully decorated holding pen. You obviously want nothing to do with me. I'm assuming you're holding me for ransom? My father won't pay anything, but Vadik Stepanov might, if only so he can rape and torture me for the inexcusable crime of being kidnapped."

That gets his attention. "You are my wife. I told you that night it would guarantee your safety. I am a man of my word."

There's an undertow to Cameron. On the surface, he's cold and composed, like still water. But when I look into his eyes, there's an inexorable pull, like the moon and the ocean tides.

He's not cold. There's heat there. And dislike. He's fighting between the two.

"I'm drifting around this house like a ghost. Can you give me something here? Anything?"

That frown is taking up permanent residence between his brows. "What is it that you think I owe you, wife?"

Why did that just send a jolt up my spine?

"Can I go back to school?" I hurry ahead before he can refuse, "I can finish my art degree online, I would just need to meet with my advisor once in Copenhagen. If your family owns any art-related businesses, I could be useful with marketing or... valuation?" I hate how unsure I sound at the end of my little speech, but there's no real reason for him to refuse me unless he's an utter and complete bastard.

"I see no reason for you to waste the time," he says coldly. "It's not a career you're going to pursue."

Just then, Miss Kevin enters with a huge tureen of soup. She stumbles. I have no idea on what, because the floor is bare, and with an expression of utter horror, she drops the tureen on the table and it splashes the silk-covered chairs. The antique walnut table.

And Cameron's bespoke suit.

Not a drop makes it all fifteen feet down the table to me, and I watch as he leaps to his feet, cursing while poor Miss Kevin apologizes profusely. Throwing his napkin into the lake of soup, he stalks out the door.

The curse of the Ivanov's strikes again.

Miss Kevin looks at me apologetically. "Would you like to have your dinner in the library?"

Leaning back, I grin at her and take a healthy gulp of wine. "I believe I would love to have my dinner right here, Miss Kevin. Thank you very much."

CHAPTER SEVEN

In which Morana is paraded out to See and Be Seen.

Morana...

The next morning...

"Let's try this again."

I look up from my book to see Cameron leaning against the library door, arms folded.

Putting my battered novel aside, I smile sweetly, thinking about the soup dumped in his lap last night. Did it burn anything important? I have no idea how big he is, but based on the size of the rest of him, he must be gigantic.

"Of course. How are you feeling?"

His eyes darken to that forest green again. "Other than an extensive dry-cleaning bill, I'm fine."

"That's good," I agree placidly. I can tell my bland smile is irritating him and that gives me such joy. "I am delighted to revisit last night's conversation with the hope that you'll reconsider my request to finish my degree."

He's watching me like he's waiting for something, some revelation. It's not that hard. I just want to go back to school.

"That's a possibility." He walks over like a GQ cover come to life and seats himself across from me. "I want you to tell me what you know about the Ivanov Bratva business."

"If that's why you kidnapped me and forced me to marry you, this will be a deeply disappointing conversation," I say. "My father hates me. He sent me off to boarding school as soon as possible. I didn't spend much time at home. Even though I was curious about why the family fortunes were declining so quickly, he would never tell a mere *woman* anything."

Cameron's brow rose. "The ancient-minded traditional Bratva?"

"Women have no place, aside from arranged marriages and having children," I say, rubbing my eyes. "He was quite clear."

"You're a smart girl, you must have had your sources of information, even so."

"My sources? Everyone in the household thought I was a curse," I chuckle bitterly. "Do you know what Morana means in Russian?"

He leans back, running his hand over the stubble on his chin. "Tell me."

"Death. It means death. My father named me Morana after my mother died in childbirth. Every time he got drunk, he'd remind me that I killed my mother. Anyone who wanted to stay in his good graces would have nothing to do with me. I know the Ivanov fortunes are failing. He was losing everything my grandfather built. My betrothal to Stepanov, that vile old troll, was his last hope."

"I'm sorry about your mother," he says, "growing up without her must have been very lonely."

It was the last thing I would ever expect from him. Empathy? Kindness?

"Th- thank you?"

He gives me a slight smile and then it's back to business. "What do you know about your - former - fiancé's Bratva?"

Shuddering, I look down, compulsively smoothing my skirt over my knees. "He's the epitome of evil, the worst of the Moscow Six Families. He steals women and children and sells them into slavery. He runs them through his clubs and bordellos. Even the other families hate him."

Cameron leaned forward, watching me closely. "Have you been to any of his clubs?"

Frowning, I shrug a little. "My father took me to *Klub Razvratnyy* for our first meeting. It was in his office above the club, though, a private entrance."

He looks puzzled for a moment before covering it with a practiced smile. "Club Depraved? Well, the name fits. We can talk about you finishing your degree."

Eyeing him suspiciously, I wait for it. He's going to hold my hopes hostage for good behavior. I've played this game before.

"There's a gala we're attending tonight at the Festival Theatre. Miss Kevin should be bringing up your dress as we speak, and a stylist is coming to help you get ready-"

My first thought is of my German jailer at my ill-fated wedding. "No! I can do my own hair and makeup, I assure you. I've been to dozens of black-tie events, I won't embarrass you."

He picks up my hand, kissing the back of it. "I have no doubt."

"You're freaking me out," I blurt. "Why are you suddenly being nice to me?"

"Well, we are married," he shrugs.

"Uh huh..." I say dubiously. "So, connect the dots between my degree and this event tonight."

"There will be a wee bit of attention at the gala," he understates. "Those who are aware of our marriage will be keen to see us together."

"And you want me to be the adoring bride?" I ask, "You're provoking Stepanov with a display like that. On the bright side, it might give my father a stroke."

Pulling me to my feet, he gives me a grin that can only be

described as rakish. "I'm thinking you're going to have a good time tonight, lass."

I'd never seen Edinburgh at night, how the spotlights glitter over the glass surface of the Festival Theatre, the red carpet, and elaborately dressed guests. The quaint, quiet beauty of the city has a harder edge.

"Is that the same tux you wore to kidnap me?" I ask, because while Cameron looks incredible and so sexy in formal wear that it's almost criminal, wearing the same suit would be such bad luck.

"No," he scowls, "my cleaner's very good with getting out blood, but I ripped the jacket."

"Are you sure this is a good idea?" I persist, as he's rapidly texting someone as we pull up to the entrance. Eyeing the buildings around us, I can spot at least six perfect places for a sniper to put a bullet in my head - or his - and be gone before anyone noticed we'd been shot.

"Aye," he says absently. "You'll have security with you at all times."

"I'm not thrilled about the idea of going in there, if I'm being honest with you."

"And I appreciate that honesty," he says, "but we're still going in." Putting away his phone, Cameron kisses my limp hand. "I promised you the protection of the MacTavish Clan when we married. I keep my word. So relax, yeah? Play your part. You might have fun tonight even if this is out of your comfort zone."

"Comfort zone?" I laugh weakly, "I'm fairly sure we left my comfort zone somewhere back in Moscow."

He winks as he helps me out of the Range Rover.

Walking up the stairs, I'm acutely aware of just how high the slit is on this dress. It's a deep violet silk, backless but at least it's covering my breasts. The silk is thin enough that I had to tape my nipples down. The combination of too much skin and not enough is tantalizing, and I'm a bit surprised he ordered it for me.

"If one thing shifts on this dress," I hiss to him, "I'm going to flash half the guests tonight."

Something glints in his eyes, and he grips my hand tightly. "I'll tear the tablecloth off the buffet and wrap you in it before I let that happen."

"The dress *was* your choice," I remind him.

"Aye, I underestimated just how well it would fit you."

His grim tone makes me laugh, and suddenly, it's possible that this night might not be a disaster after all.

CHAPTER EIGHT

In which we meet in-laws and unsettling billionaires.

Cameron...

My plan tonight was simple: show off my wife.

It works better than I'd expected. If one more arsehole tries to look down her dress as I introduce her, I'm going to punch their teeth in.

"Brother!" Cormac strolls up to me and I yank the drink out of his hand, downing it. "Really, you bastard? Ya' can't get your own?" His mouth turns down a bit as he turns to Morana, and I step between them. I'm not sure why. I know he wouldn't hurt her, but his expression, the barely concealed distaste... she doesn't deserve it.

"At last! We meet!" Mala steps up, smiling warmly. "You must be Morana, *rad vstreche,* nice to meet you. I'm Mala, married to this grim-looking Scotsman here. Sweetheart, have you introduced yourself yet?"

"I was just about to," he says, still reserved but slightly more pleasant. "Cormac MacTavish, a pleasure to meet you, Morana."

"*Spasibo,* thank you," she says. Her smile is tight and she's edging a little closer to me. That I'm her safest port in this social storm is spiking me with unfamiliar feelings. Like guilt.

Putting my arm around her, I can feel her relax incrementally. "Mala, I didn't know you spoke Russian."

"*Nemnogo,*" Mala says, "just a little. Forgive my atrocious accent,

Morana."

"Not at all," my bride says, "it's nice to hear it again."

Cormac is looking down at her with a slight thawing, like he'd expected a pit viper but ended up with a bunny.

My brother always looks intimidating, whether he's feeling that way or no. He's as tall and broad as I am, and standing next to Mala, they make a striking couple. I can objectively say my sister-in-law is beautiful, with her dark auburn hair and blue eyes, even though she is relentlessly annoying.

Mala loops her arm through Morana's and pulls her toward the buffet tables. "Don't worry about them," she says, "they'll talk business and bore the hell out of us. Meanwhile, I am certain I saw lobster wontons over there." Morana gives a little smile and looks over her shoulder at me.

"Grab a couple of those wontons for me," I grin.

When I turn back to my brother, he's staring at me with a frown. "That all had a newlywed ring to it. I thought you were keeping your distance."

"I think Nikandr is wrong," I say, and I realize that I believe it. "I don't see it. We've seen some slick actresses in this business, but she's got no guile."

Shaking his head, he asks, "Are you sure you're not just seeing what you want to see? She's a bonny lass, that. But she's also the rich, pampered princess of a piece of shite like Ivanov."

"Not so rich," I murmur angrily, "that's why just draining the rest of his money isn't enough."

Cormac's watching his wife, laughing and talking with mine, eyes narrowed. I know how protective he is of Mala, but I don't like how he's looking at Morana as if she's a disease that could infect her.

"Talk to Nikandr again," I say. "Make sure he's clear on what he saw, aye?"

He looks doubtful, but he nods. "Let's get back to the women before I have to stab those slimy fecks who are moving in on them."

I don't bother to tell him that the well-dressed couple standing next to them are from my security staff. I'd hired the blonde Norwegian husband and wife team because they are less conspicuous than the standard giant fuckers most of us in the business use. The woman, Natalia, can serve as a personal bodyguard for Morana when I finally let her out of the house on her own. I watch with a grin as Natalia and Sven casually pivot in front of the two men heading for our wives, blocking them from moving in.

We walk through the crowd, shaking hands and deftly sidestepping a couple of lower-level thugs, desperate for a connection with our clan.

"Keep an eye on the Lord Provost," Cormac murmurs. "If he even looks like he's turning toward those Blackwood arseholes, we'll cut that connection with a fecking ax if necessary."

"We haven't used a hatchet in a long time," I reminisce, "remember those two pricks from the Triad attack? You pulled *Sean-seanair's* ceremonial battle-axe right off the wall."

"Aye," he agrees, "it fit the moment. Hell of a mess to clean up, though."

I don't see the woman with the enormous chest barely encased in her red dress until she nearly falls into me, grabbing at my jacket.

"Oh, pardon! I'm such a *stammerel-* so clumsy. Cameron, is that you, darlin'?"

Staring at her, I'm trying to place a name to the tits. Those, I recognize, which is likely why she's shoving them in my face.

"Lorna Buchanan, silly! We spent some time together last

summer? How lovely to run into you!"

Glancing over her shoulder, I see that Mala and Morana are still deep in discussion, while my new wife may not make a fuss, my sister-in-law would never let me live this down. The very purpose of her existence is to remind me of my past indiscretions.

"Of course," I say, stepping backward. She nearly falls into me again, off-balance. Cormac, that bastard, is just watching this unfold with a barely hidden grin. "How are you?"

I'm thinking I met her at one of our clubs in Glasgow. I was pretty scuppered and my hazy memory recalls that we used the office above the club to fuck.

"I'm so good," she purrs, "just in town for a photo shoot."

"Uh, huh…" I check Morana's location over her shoulder again.

"We should get together while I'm here, you can show me around?" Lorna's persistent, I'll give her that.

"My apologies, I'm certain my wife would not appreciate it," I say, watching her practiced smile fade.

"Married? You?" Her eyes are narrowing as she gives a little giggle. "I've heard no such thing."

"He's just newly wed," Cormac finally throws me a fecking bone and steps in. "He swept his lovely bride right off her feet and stole… her heart."

Bastard.

"Given your history, lad, it's surprising she recognized you without your dick out," he chuckles as we walk away.

Just as we reach our women, Alain Baird, the Lord Provost of Edinburgh greets us. "It can't be!" he says in a carrying voice meant to deliver a rousing campaign speech, "Cameron MacTavish married? There's an entire city of women in mourning tonight, I'm certain."

Morana turns with an uncomfortable smile and I take her left hand, lifting it to show him. "I'm happy to say I am." I give him a large grin with too many teeth. "My beautiful bride, Morana Ivanova MacTavish."

I don't like Baird's speculative stare, but he's courteous and charming to my bride and I move her away as soon as is polite.

"Are you having fun?" I murmur in her ear as I slide my arm around her waist. Sweet Jesus, this dress is too thin, the silk is warm from her body and I can feel the muscles in her back move as she shifts to look up at me, eyes wide in surprise.

"Yes," she admits, "Mala is so nice! She was just telling me about meeting your brother at the Ares Academy."

"Ya' mean when my cradle-robbing brother carried off one of his students?"

Cormac glares at me. "I didn't carry her off, arsehole."

"Well, you really did," corrects Mala. "I mean, I had no idea what was happening when I walked onto your jet. I thought I was marrying that wife-murdering Don in Los Angeles."

"What?" Morana gasps, and I get to enjoy my brother's sour expression as Mala tells the story of how she met *Professor* MacTavish at the Academy and they carried on an affair before he made a better deal with her arsehole da' for her hand in marriage. I'm one of the very few who knows they first met for what was, apparently, an incredible night in London before school started.

After a couple of minutes, I realize my fingers have slipped under Morana's dress and I'm stroking her back. I can feel the silk of her panties and the smooth skin above them, a slight dip just above her ass... are those dimples?

A pointed throat clearing from my brother makes me look up. He and Mala are trying not to laugh. Morana hasn't moved, but the high color on her cheeks shows she's not unaffected by my touch.

"We're dancing," I say, abruptly pulling her away from my idiot family.

Out on the dance floor, I can spread my hand wide against the bare skin of her back and pull her close. "Have I mentioned how much I like this dress?"

"If I'd known it was chosen for its easy access points, I would have put a sweater over it," Morana mutters.

Another couple bumps into us.

"Cameron MacTavish, you're a large enough target that I'm surprised we bumped into you."

"Nolan O'Rourke? I was just drinking a bottle from your twenty-five-year cask the other night," I said, holding out my hand.

O'Rourke is an enigma, even in our world where no one is what they seem. He's blond, and model-handsome, in his late forties but looks younger. He's made billions in real estate investments all over the world, but his real power is as an information broker. Unfortunately, getting intel from him almost always costs more than it's worth.

He chuckles indulgently, taking the handshake. His gaze slices over to Morana immediately. "Why darling, you're far from home."

She stiffens against me. "Have we met?"

"No, but I know your father and fiancé - well, *former* fiancé," he smiles pleasantly.

"Do you do business with them?" She's pale and I feel her shaking, but her lips are set firm in a tight line.

"Not the sort you're thinking of, dear."

She relaxes slightly, but I know she's still rattled. Guiding her over to the side of the floor, I nod to my bodyguards. "Morana, this is Natalia, she will be part of your security detail. Do you need to freshen up?"

Morana's narrowed glance darts between me and O'Rourke, but she nods reluctantly and walks away with Natalia.

Swinging back to O'Rourke, I go on the attack. "What are you playing at?"

He lifted one haughty brow, "I don't know what you mean, Cameron. I'm merely greeting old acquaintances."

"Do you know my wife?" I leaned closer, suddenly furious at the thought, but O'Rourke is both a billionaire and slightly insane, so he's not disturbed in the least.

"I don't believe I've ever met her formally, her father used to keep her under lock and key," he drawls, "but of course, Moscow society was looking forward to the spectacle of her wedding to Vadik Stepanov. You quite stole his thunder. I understand he's rather displeased about it."

Tilting my head, I watch him for a moment. I know this man is a sociopath, and he enjoys his games, but there's no one better connected. "Do you have a financial interest with either Bratva?"

"Not at this time," he shrugs, "I am not interested in human trafficking. So much fuss."

"Then you're neither gaining or losing by my recent marriage, yet you went out of your way to unsettle my wife."

"I did hear the rumors, but with that rather noticeable ring on her hand and your affectionate - though a tad possessive - behavior tonight, that should settle everyone's speculations." He brushed a speck of lint off his perfect black tux. "I do hope you have a plan, because there is a firestorm coming your way."

"When I'm finished," I say softly, "there will be nothing left of those families but ash, and bone."

O'Rourke's looking for something, he searches my eyes for a

moment and then nods as if it's all settled. "I would not bet against you, MacTavish. Give my best to your new bride. Goodnight."

CHAPTER NINE

In which Morana gets to know her security with an uncomfortable visit to the Panic Room.

Morana...

"Who was *that* spooky man?"

We're driving home and for a change, Cameron is not ignoring me and glued to his phone. He knew who I meant right away.

"Nolan O'Rourke, I didn't get a chance to introduce you properly. He's a billionaire and a bit mad."

"Who looks like a supermodel," I murmur, "if the supermodel was a serial killer."

"I'm thinking I should question that further, but movin' on. He does business with everyone in the crime world. He's associated with every organization but allied with none of them," Cameron explained, "he's the only man I've seen who can move around like that with no consequences."

"How did he know who I was? I'm sure I've never met him before."

He runs a hand through his hair, smiling wryly. "Nolan knows everything and everyone. He enjoys stirring up trouble and knocking people off balance. But his presence tonight plays in our favor. The word will be out by midnight that we are married and you are off the table as a bargaining chip."

The fact that he added that last bit made me unexpectedly emotional. I know he hadn't done any of this to protect me, but still. He had promised that I would be safe as his wife. My father couldn't use me anymore.

I give him the first real smile I've had since I was taken. It's on the tip of my tongue to thank him and I shut up in time. He did take me from what promised to be a genuinely horrible future. But I don't know this man. I don't know what his game is, other than wanting to destroy my father's Bratva. And he could be planning to make me a part of that destruction in a way that will burn me to ash, too.

The rest of the drive is silent, and he helps me out of the car back at the house. *His house,* I remind myself. The lights are dimmed, aside from the two-story entryway. I'm so used to having Miss Kevin bustling around, and the standard bristle of bodyguards that the silence is unsettling.

"Have a drink with me."

It's less of a suggestion and more of an order from Cameron, but he's in an oddly soft mood.

"I hear this has turned into your favorite room in the house," he says, pouring me a glass of wine from the bar in the library.

"How could it not be?" I scoff, "This is library porn at its finest!"

"Library porn?" he laughs, "What the hell?"

"You know, Pinterest-worthy? The perfect mix of books and couches, the correct ratio of elegant wood paneling to majestic windows? The built-in window seat is so perfect that I would live in here if you let me."

Cameron's never really laughed around me, and *blin,* damn it, it just makes him hotter. He throws his head back and I admire his beautifully sculpted profile. I'm used to spiteful snickers, or the uneasy laughter my father's sycophants give for anything they think might be meant as funny. But this man laughs heartily, like he doesn't care who hears him, his hugely muscled chest heaving.

Gulping my wine, I hold out my glass for a refill, hoping he'll have another drink, too. Can I possibly get him drunk, loosen him up a little? Maybe I can dig out more information about what's in store for me.

A Russian and a Scotsman, I think wryly, *it's a fair fight.*

Two more glasses of wine and I'm giggling about an explanation of the Scottish insults that Cameron and his brothers used to trade back and forth.

"So, when Dougal said, 'Yer bum's oot the windae, ye fuckin' bampot,' he was saying 'You're talking rubbish, you unhinged tit.'"

I'm laughing hard enough that getting my breath back is next to impossible, so when the lights go out, I can only give a startled wheeze. My hands reach out, searching for Cameron, and he takes my hand when I find him.

"Just an outage, lass. We have a backup generator, no fear."

"Does your security system and the outdoor lights still work?" I whisper, my heart thudding painfully in my chest. This is more than an outage. Is it the Stepanov Bratva? My psychotic cousin? Cameron has enemies, I'm sure.

With a long whine, the lights go on again and I hear electronics booting back up.

"Lass, you're pale as pudding."

I realize how close I am to Cameron when he cups my face in his huge hands. "Just an outage, Morana. And my security system is on a separate power source."

Nodding a little too fast, I try to swallow past my dry throat. His forest-colored eyes are fixed on mine, he's still cradling my face. If he leaned down an inch or two, he could kiss me.

"Boss? We have an issue."

Hamish is standing just outside in the hall, not quite looking at us as if we might be naked or something.

"Call Natalia to accompany my wife up to her bedroom. She does not leave her for any reason," Cameron says, releasing me and heading for the door without looking back.

Natalia is already waiting for me. "Mrs. MacTavish?"

Hitching up the skirts of this ridiculous silk dress, I hurry after her.

"What do you know, Natalia?"

I'm standing in a corner of my bedroom that gives me some view of the grounds around the house without standing directly in front of a window, which she instantly stopped.

"The power outage was intentional," she says, her gun out, held like an extension of her hand. She's so strong and competent that she looks out of place in the floral delicacy of this room. "No one has breached the grounds, I assure you that you're safe." She's not looking at me as she talks, I get the feeling she may not like me much. I get what she thinks she sees, a spoiled rich girl. Soft. Weak.

"Do you think you could teach me how to shoot?" I blurt.

Now she glances over. "Ma'am, I don't think-"

"I'll ask Cameron, of course," I interrupt, "but... I hate being helpless. I'm sure he wouldn't say no to some self-defense training. Wouldn't I be less of a liability if I had some skills?"

She's hesitating, I can see it. "I don't know if Mr. MacTavish would want you to..."

It hits me. "Oh. He doesn't trust me, does he?" The carefully blank expression on her face tells me what I need to know. "All right. I'm just going to change out of this dress."

"Please be quick, ma'am, just in case I have to move you from this location." Natalia nods politely, back to scanning the grounds below us.

Hastily sliding into some jeans and sneakers, I feel a sickening sense of certainty that this has to do with my father. I'm a little shocked that he came after me, he's not the type to expend the cost and effort. I'm useless to his plans now, no longer his virginal Bratva princess.

There's a shatter of glass below us and a huge 'whoosh!' as a wall of fire goes up against the house. I can see the flames' shadows on the wall as Natalia yanks me down the hall. There's shouting and Cameron's voice rises above the others, calling out directions.

"Where are we going?" I try to pull my arm away, but she has a death grip on my arm like I'm a toddler who can't be trusted to follow her. She picks up speed, taking the corner at a run and nearly sling-shotting me into the opposite wall. I see a door that's wider and taller than the others down the hall and it's clear it's a safe room. There's a heavy 'thunk!' as the steel door closes behind us.

A bank of monitors in front of us lights up as the door closes. She's ignoring me now and moving through the different security camera shots, tracking the action. The flames are distorting two of the camera angles, but I can see Cameron shooting at someone behind the scant shelter of one of the granite pillars in front.

"Whoever it is used the firebomb in back as a distraction to break right through the gates, smart." I nod absently. Natalia looks at me with well-bred disgust. "This is horrible and I'm praying it's not my father," I say, trying to shove down my frustration, "believe me, I hope that whoever is attacking the house meets a very swift end."

Keeping my mouth shut, I watch the action as the gunfire quickly dies down, as well as the flames, there's bodies dragged off to the north corner of the back garden and I hope they're not Cameron's people. I hope that no one dies because of me.

Finally escorted back to my room, Natalia locks me in. I want to pound on the door and demand to see Cameron, but I hang on to my temper by my fingernails. He's dealing with the aftermath of an attack on his home. The last person who is owed an update is me, especially if it came from my father.

It's Miss Kevin who unlocks my door the next morning with breakfast and her usual elegant smile.

"Can you please tell me what happened last night?" I plead.

As always, she won't sit down with me, but she nods sympathetically. "The bodies don't point to any known group, but two of them bear the tattoos of an Albanian squad known for being hired out to do the…" her nose wrinkles slightly, "dirty work."

"Did Cameron lose any men?" She lays out a cloth napkin on my lap with great ceremony and I'm so frustrated by her magnificent, glacial pace that I'm about to twirl it and snap her on the ass with it. "Was he hurt? Was anyone hurt?"

"There were a couple of injuries," she allowed. "Master MacTavish was not hurt."

"What about the damage from the fire?" She's standing there, looking pointedly at my sausages, fried eggs, and tomatoes.

First Natalia and now her? Everyone here thinks I'm a toddler.

With a sigh, I pick up my fork and stab at a morsel of egg.

"The damage was minimal," she says, "it was put out almost instantly. The window was replaced this morning. Really, the annoyance from the neighbors is more tiresome to deal with."

Picturing Cameron shouting over his fifteen-foot wall at an irate neighbor almost makes me laugh until I remember how helpless

I felt last night.

"I want to learn how to defend myself, and Natalia refused, indicating that Cameron wouldn't allow it. How would you handle this?" Miss Kevin is the only one in this house who doesn't seem either afraid of, or disgusted by me.

"Well…" she allowed, "I would not presume to put myself in your place. But I do feel that sometimes strong emotions, such as anger, can be a compelling addition to one's argument. It is not always helpful to be demure and ladylike in a Scottish family."

I question if I am either of those things, but a grin stretches across my face. "Miss Kevin, you are my personal hero and guiding light."

One elegant brow arches, "That is rather a lot to expect, but I shall endeavor to live up to your vision, Madame Morana."

CHAPTER TEN

In which Morana is vanilla pudding and Cameron is dark chocolate whorebag.

Cameron...

When my bride walks into the gym the next morning, her anger is almost big enough to enter first.

"Why won't you let me learn to defend myself!"

Giving a nod, I watch my lieutenants who had been working out with me scatter from the room like roaches under a flashlight.

Morana's fists are clenched as she storms over to me and I wonder if she's ever thrown a punch before.

"Really, what can you possibly be afraid of? That I'll shoot you? Stab you in your sleep? I'm not even completely sure *where* you sleep in this place! I just want-" She pushes all that thick blonde hair out of her face, trying to get the words out. "I just don't want to be helpless when they come for me!"

At first, I'm insulted that she thinks I'd let Stepanov or that bastard father of hers come near her. Did she listen at all when I gave her my word to protect her?

"Okay then..." I take the tape off my knuckles, pulling off my shirt to wipe the sweat off my face. As I throw it away, I notice she's staring at my chest, her pretty violet eyes wide. "Let's do some work."

"Huh?" She flushes painfully as her gaze darts back up to mine. "You'll let Natalia teach me?"

"She's doing some work for me right now, and I'm available," I say, spreading my arms out to indicate the empty gym. She bites her lip and the sight makes me groan silently. I want to be the one biting that lip, running my tongue along the seam of her mouth and-

Concentrate, ye' arsehole!

"What level are you at now?" I ask, "What kind of training did your bodyguards give you?"

Her mouth tightens, and she won't meet my eyes. "None."

"They didn't teach you any self-defense or evasion tactics at all?" I ask incredulously. Everyone in the MacTavish Clan, young and old, male and female, learned hand-to-hand combat and proficiency with at least one weapon.

"No," she snaps, "it was forbidden. I'm pretty sure my father wanted to keep me as weak as possible."

Her father's a fool. There's nothing weak about Morana.

"Then let's start with some basics," I nodded. I beckoned her closer with two fingers. "On the mat."

Kicking off her shoes, she steps closer, rubbing her hands on her yoga pants. I think that's what they're called. All I know is they're tight and stretchy and frame her spectacular arse. Too well. I should insist that she can't wear them around anyone but me.

"Here's some basic points, as a beginner. One of the quickest ways to incapacitate an attacker is with the nose or throat punch. You're left-handed, so hold up that hand and flex your wrist a little."

She's so serious, it's almost endearing.

"Now, you're going to use the heel of your hand to strike." Taking her by the wrist, I show her the move. "The trick is to recoil your strike, pulling your arm back quickly builds the momentum that'll knock the attacker's head up and back."

We practice the move for a few minutes, and she's so focused that I get to enjoy the curls coming loose from her ponytail, and the excitement radiating from her. The late afternoon sun is slanting through the windows, highlighting her glowing skin.

"Good girl," I praise her, watching her cheeks turn pink. "Next, let's work on the elbow strike," I try to focus. "You, with those pointy elbows of yours, they're already a deadly weapon."

"Pointy?" she says, "Pointy?" Holding up said elbow, she looks at me disapprovingly. "They're not any pointier than yours."

"If you say so," I laugh, "but they're quite useful as weapons if you're too close to set up a kick or punch. Plant yer' feet, get stable…"

I'm nearly certain she didn't mean to angle her elbow down instead of up, but that sharp, pointy bit of her hits me right in the goods.

Seventy percent sure she didn't mean to.

"Oh, *bozhe moy* I'm sorry!" she says, waving her hands like fluttering birds around me, trying to help but not daring to touch me, which is wise. "I didn't mean- really, I'm so sorry!"

"This is a good time for a water break," I say, when I've recovered my voice.

It's not the first time I've been hit below the belt during a sparring session, so we start again. Carefully.

The sun is setting when I teach her one of my favorite moves, and not just because I can get my hands on her.

"Ya' need a break? Do you want to sit down?"

She shakes her head, drinking half a bottle of water at my insistence. My bride is down to her sports bra and those tight, stretchy pants and it's going to be impossible to hide the fact that my dick's hard enough to pull down my zipper. How he had recovered from the incident not an hour ago is a testament to just how beautiful my bride is.

"Ye' use this move on an attack from behind, when a man tries to lock ye' down with a bear hug. It's a harder one to defend against," I say hoarsely.

"Okay," she nods firmly, absolutely focused.

"The second you're grabbed, you bend from the waist. Shift your weight forward and make it harder for your attacker to pick you up. You've got a wee bit of space between ye', enough to bring an elbow back to their face or neck. Ready?"

"Uh-huh." She trustingly puts her back to me and I groan silently, seeing that perfect arse on display again.

"I'm puttin' my arms around you now," I warn, trying to keep my hips angled so my cock doesn't dig into her back, but the moment she leans forward, she freezes.

"I only have so much self-control, lass," I say, "and your arse is very distractin'."

She turns around in the circle of my arms, looking up at me. I can't seem to loosen my grip. Goddamn, her breasts are pressed hard against my chest and I can feel the taut little points of her nipples pushing against the thin spandex between us.

"Why haven't you tried to have sex with me?" Morana blurts in that adorable way she has, eyes widening after she speaks as if that's not what she'd planned to say at all.

"I'm a consent kind of man," I say, enjoying the feel of her perfect little nipples. "I'm progressive like that."

Her brows draw together. "You're fine with kidnapping me and forcing me to marry you, but you draw the line at having sex with me?"

"Do you want me to have sex with you, *mo fhlùr?*" Pressing my cock against her stomach, I can feel her deep breath. I can't hold back. I can't stay away from my wife any longer, no matter who she was before I took her. "Do you want me to slide into you? Fill you up? Lick your nipples and bite them, spank that perfect arse?"

"Wh- I-" Her lips are attempting to shape words, but she's having trouble, so I halt the effort by kissing her, groaning in relief and grabbing a fistful of her hair, holding her still.

It's dark in the gym now, the sun's set, and no lights switched on, so it's easy to be honest. "I fecking want you, lass," I whisper into her ear, giving it a sharp bite, enjoying how she jumps a little. "I've been desperate to get inside you since the moment I married you."

"Against my will," she manages to protest before I kiss her again.

"You get this choice," I softly tug on her lower lip with my teeth. "You can tell me yes-" I grip her arse and bring her up hard against my cock and she gives a deeply satisfying moan. "Or no." Dropping her back to her feet, I hold her as she staggers, regaining her balance. Even in the shadows, her eyes are glowing and she's so beautiful. So exquisite.

"I'm not going to be any good at this," she warns me. "I'm vanilla pudding and you- you're a dark chocolate whorebag."

Howling with laughter, I lean over enough to throw her over my shoulder, slapping her arse with a thunderous strike as I race out of the gym and up the long flight of stairs to my room.

CHAPTER ELEVEN

In which Morana melts faster than butter in a microwave.

Morana...

Upside down and watching Cameron's ass flex with every step he takes, I wonder if I've been catapulted into an alternate reality because I'm pretty sure he doesn't like me. He definitely doesn't trust me but now he's shoving open a set of double doors I've never entered before.

So, this is the master bedroom...

As I view it from upside down, I see the huge walnut four-poster bed he's heading for, not the slightest bit winded by loping up the stairs with me like a panther.

"Ah!"

I'm right side up again and kneeling on the bed, it's one of those high, high mattresses that you need a little footstool by the side of the bed to climb up on it. My husband and I are almost eye to eye.

"I need you to say the words, lass." His gesture of consent is weakened a bit by the fact that he's pulling off my bra at the same time, and any thought of saying 'no' just to spite him disappears as his lips eagerly fasten onto my nipple.

"That's..." My hands are in his hair suddenly and I'm lightly scratching his scalp, holding his head to me. His teeth gently bite it as his tongue soothes the burn. *"Bozhe moy,* oh my god," I moan.

"Say..." he kisses that nipple and then the other one, the tip of his tongue trailing up my throat, "...the words. Do you want this?" He licks his lips like a predator at the top of the food chain.

"Are we really married?"

The words hang in the air, almost tangible and I realize that I've doubted it all along, that this ring on my finger is no more real than the words he forced me to speak in front of the priest.

And he has the effrontery to look offended.

"How many women do you think I bring home and bribe our parish priest to marry? Do you remember the license you signed along with me and Father Barclay? Miss Kevin was the witness if you need to double-check with her. This ring-" he holds up my hand, forcing me to look at the diamond glittering on it, "this is real. Our union is real." He taps his ring against mine, a simple silver one that suits his enormous hand.

"Yes, please," I manage to get the words out that my body has been screaming for the last hour. "I want you."

"Thank Christ," he says before kissing me fiercely again, his long, capable fingers smoothing down over my stomach and between my legs. His rough, calloused fingertips are stroking through my lips, already wet and he growls. "Why, sweet lass, you're already wet, aren't you? So silky..." He slides down and there's a jolt like an electrical charge surging through my center as his hot mouth fastens over me. I can feel him tugging my leggings off, then using his fingers to spread me open.

He growls again, and it vibrates through me, making me suck in a breath, my knees drawing up. Impatiently shoving them apart with his broad shoulders, he licks me, long, like a cat with the flat of his tongue and then tickles my clitoris with his tongue, circling it delicately, then more firmly as I moan, my hands over my face.

This is so much, it's all so much and the heat of his mouth, the heavy weight of him pinning me down is good and overwhelming and I never want him to stop. When I feel his tongue drive up inside me, his thumb circling my clitoris, I'm shocked into an orgasm. That's how it feels, something overwhelming, crashing in on me and like nothing any exploration that my own fingers have managed.

"Your sweet as candy pussy is going to kill me," he rasps, "I was going to go slow with you, take more time with my tongue. But now you have to wait for that, because I'm at my breaking point."

Rearing up, he pulls off his shirt, revealing a colorful array of tattoos; daggers and angel's wings, a snarling lion's head.

And then he does something that melts me faster than butter in the microwave. His hand swipes down my wet center, slicking up his palm, and he strokes it over his dick, like he wants to feel my slick on him. There's the faint crinkle of a wrapper and his fingers deftly rolling a condom down his length.

There's a weak, inarticulate sound escaping my slack lips as Cameron lifts me by my waist, sliding under me and making me straddle him as he leans against the headboard. Notching the broad head of his cock inside me, he chuckles darkly. "So hot inside, aren't you, wife? An inferno." Then he lowers me and I'm stretching around him, *bozhe moy,* he's bigger than I thought he could be and it stings and burns and it's so good. So much better than I could have imagined.

My nails dig into his shoulders, trying to gain some balance but I'm still sliding down this massive thing inside me and he's murmuring filthy words in my ear, and knowing that this is affecting him just as much makes me wetter. He drops me, the last several inches shoving inside me and I'm impaled on his lap. My breath's coming out in little gasps and wheezes and he chuckles, sounding a little breathless himself.

"There we go," he whispers diabolically, "such a pretty, sweet girl taking every inch of me and still so wet. Have you been thinking of this? Dirty dreams about my cock between your legs?" His strong hands lift me halfway off his shaft and drops me again, and this time I shriek. "Come on," he urges hoarsely, "I know you can take all of me."

"I'm trying," I moan, it hurts when he buries every inch of that massive dick inside me, and it sends heat flaring under my skin, all through me, and then the next thick thrust, and the next and all I can do is moan deliriously.

On the next downward thrust, my clitoris rubs against something hard and I gasp, looking down. "What is- what is that?" There's a barbell piercing at the base of his shaft, it's placed perfectly to press against me on every thrust and my whole body stiffens like I've been struck by lightning.

"It's for you, lass." With a devilish smile, Cameron angles his hips up, hitting right against my defenseless clitoris again and I shriek. Flipping me over onto my back, he drives back into me. "Beautiful," he groans, "so feckin' beautiful, wife. I'm going to make certain this perfect little pussy remembers who she belongs to. Come again, *mo fhlùr.*"

"I- I don't think I can." Gasping and shaking, I can feel him all the way through my body, every part taken over by his thick shaft pounding into me.

"You can," he whispers, Lucifer in the flesh, hovering over me like a dark angel, his eyes greedily watching me. "Let go."

"I can't."

"You can," he promises, lifting my ass with his hand, driving into me at a slightly different angle, even deeper and he's right.

I come again.

With a groan, he thrusts into me three more times, pushing deep and holding there, his head dropping to my shoulder. He gathers me in his arms, rolling to the side, still buried inside me with his leg thrown over mine. I'm enclosed in this fortress of beautiful flesh and muscle and for the first time I can ever remember, I feel safe.

Reality returns when Cameron gently pulls his cock out of me. He looks down, frowning. "Ah, shite. I didn't intend to hurt you. Or are you on your cycle?"

It takes me a minute to realize what he's saying. "You didn't know I was- this was my first time." Saying 'You didn't know you deflowered me?' seems painfully awkward, given what we've just done.

His expression changes from startled to remorseful in seconds. "Sweet Jesus, I should have been more careful with ya'. I'd forgotten that the Bratva girls are expected to be pure, which is the stupidest feckin' thing."

I forget my embarrassment. "Really? You wouldn't have demanded your wife be, you know..."

"Virgin?" he finished. "Why the hell shouldn't you have the same right to decide who you want to fuck and what you like? The only reason these old bastards insist on a virgin is because they're shite in bed and don't want her to have anything to compare their flaccid dicks to."

I have no frame of reference for this. I know other girls in my position, all of us expected to be untouched while the men in our Bratvas were allowed to be as whorish as they liked.

Strolling into the bathroom, he returns with a soft cloth, cleaning me despite my embarrassed protests that I could do it myself. "All that said," he muses, eyeing my center, "I dinna' expect how it would feel to be the only man inside you. Good." He leans forward and very gently licks me. "Feral."

My hand falls to the back of his thick hair as he gives me another long, slow lick. "Poor, swollen cunny. Let me make you feel better."

Cameron does, his insistence on 'making me feel better' wrings another orgasm from my exhausted self. He's being exceptionally sweet, maybe to make up for taking my virginity, though I didn't think I could have possibly enjoyed it more.

Rolling me to my side again, he settles against the curve of my ass. "I'm going to be your only, wife. But I promise to show you so many things." His voice deepens alarmingly and I give a little groan. "You'll have plenty of time to decide what you like."

CHAPTER TWELVE

In which there is a war council and we are introduced to Bad Cat.

Cameron...

Yawning as I log onto a Zoom call with my brothers, I eye my coffee and hope the caffeine kicks in as quickly as possible. Staying up all night with a beautiful woman was easier at twenty-two than it is at thirty-two.

Not that I regretted a moment of it.

"Morning brothers," Cormac says, "Dougal and Lachlan, ya' both look like you're still scuppered. Sobriety is mandatory for all future meetings."

"We're not!" Lachlan protests, "We were up all night covering that shipment from yer wife's da'. The arsehole pissed off the Blackwoods and they were planning to take it as retaliation."

"*Now*, we're drinking," Dougal says, handing him a lager and tapping his against it in a toast.

"That feckin' gobshite," groaned Cormac, rubbing his eyes. "I'll give him a call and scare the shite out of him."

When Cormac managed to break Mala's arranged marriage to Don Accardi, the weaselly prick, he had to give her father - head of the Chandler Syndicate - access to our best shipping routes on the Atlantic. He's been a thorn in our backsides ever since.

"We've been wanting to shove our feet up the collective arse of the Blackwood mob for years," I say, "I don't care what Chandler did, they know better than stepping foot in our territory."

"And you, brother," Cormac grins, "look *far founert,* near beat to shite. How are things with you and your lovely bride?"

Tucked up in bed with a broken pussy, courtesy of my cock.

"My wife is fine and none of your business. Moving on to our little project in Moscow, I might have a new ally."

Cormac leans forward and even Dougal and Lachlan put their beer bottles down. "I ran into Nolan O'Rourke at the fundraising gala the other night."

"What was the fundraiser for?" Lachlan asks.

"I dinna' know," I shrug, "but we donated to it. Back to O'Rourke. He bumped into Morana and me when we were dancing and made it clear he knew who she was. It shook her up a little."

"O'Rourke's a billionaire because his net worth is information," Cormac says, "but he's a feckin' nightmare to deal with."

"Agreed, but I contacted him yesterday and we had a discussion about trading information for logistics," I say. "The Stepanov and Ivanov Bratva's human trade is successful only because of their impressive network of ports, shipping facilities and railways. Locations that could be used for far better purposes and as such, of interest to a man like O'Rourke. He knows them all, every bolt hole, every hideaway, every place those *bratach salach,* those dirty bastards can go."

Cormac's listening intently, eyes narrowed in thought. "It's warfare tactics. We keep driving them in the direction of where they think they're safest, divesting them of assets and their captives along the way."

"I'm beginnin' to think you're not such an idiot after all," Lachlan says, giving me a grin. He's the youngest of us and has apparently forgotten the well-deserved thrashings of his youth. The smile I give him is filled with enough malice to make his grin fade.

The meeting is ending as I hear a knock on the door.

"Aye, come in."

It's Morana, wearing soft leggings and a big green sweater and looking delicious. Remembering the taste of her is making my chapped, overworked cock rise again.

"Miss Kevin and I were wondering if you'd like breakfast," she says, pushing her sleeves up and looking anywhere but at me.

"Now lass, you're not feeling shy?" I'm trying not to leer like the lecherous bastard I feel like right now.

"No!" she scoffs, still not looking at me.

"Why don't you come over here and say that again," I grin.

Now, she glares at me, trying to march over to my desk. Given the shape her pussy's in, it's more like aggressive limping. Hands on her hips, she gives me her best haughty expression. She looks magnificent. Like a Tsarina addressing an unruly mob.

"Are you having breakfast with me or not? I'm not here for you to perve over me," she says.

"So, you're not giving me a look that says you've taken an edible and I look like a chocolate cake?" My hands slide up her thighs, settling on her hips, my thumb moving over to stroke the soft leggings covering my favorite part of her. "How do you feel this morning? Still sore?"

Her hips shift slightly, making my cock harder and I smother a groan. "I'm fine," she says quickly. She pauses. "Maybe a little sore."

"Do you want me to-"

"No! No, husband, I do not want you to make me feel better because that's how this happened in the first place!" She's trying to pull away from me, but not really putting in any effort.

"Poor darlin'," I soothe, "first, breakfast and then a long soak in the hot tub."

"You have a hot tub?" she asks weakly. One hand is sliding into my hair and I know with just a few more circles of my thumb on this firm little clit...

"Aye," I groan, releasing her. "Breakfast it is."

Morana...

Cameron leaves after breakfast, wrapped in a bespoke suit that fits those broad shoulders of his like a caress. I'm feeling dangerously soft after last night, so when he pulls me in for a slightly lecherous kiss in front of Miss Kevin, I don't fight him.

There's some commotion outside as he's trying to leave, and I hear Hamish apologetically explaining that two of the Range Rovers refused to start.

Cameron stares in fury at the deeply apologetic garage master, who looks terrified. He wouldn't shoot the poor man just because the cars broke down, would he?

"The Range Rovers are brand new," Miss Kevin's impeccable skin shows a tiny frown for a microsecond before settling into her usual pleasant smile.

Growling, my husband gets into a vintage Porsche and roars off as the last working SUV with four guards follows him. Five minutes after the gates close, both stalled SUVs are running perfectly.

Leaving the puzzled garage master to commiserate with Miss Kevin, I go for a walk around the grounds. I'm sore enough that I'm worried I might not walk properly again if I can't get my muscles loosened up. Cameron making me "feel better" last night led to another round of vigorous sex on the couch, so vigorous that the leg broke, sending us both to the floor. He was still inside me at the time and the scream I let out as I came will make me cringe for the rest of my life.

Natalia is tailing me, walking about twenty feet behind me. I would invite her to walk together, but I don't think she likes me. The look she gave me the night of the Gala when I asked to train with her… polite impatience mixed with a little contempt. It stung.

There's a huge oak tree in the back of the house with a swing, I gingerly seat myself with a wince, pushing myself back and forth with my feet.

"Rowr."

I look around me, trying to find the source of the croaky, irritable complaint.

"Rowr!"

"There you are…" It's a cat. I think. It has a long, nearly naked tail with a spiky tuft at the end. Its fur is an aggressive orange and it's glaring at me, hiding under a huge lavender bush. One golden eye is at half-mast.

"Did I take your seat?"

"Who are you speaking to, Mrs. MacTavish?"

Perfect. Natalia is listening to me talk to a cat. How far I've fallen.

"The cat. It looks pretty rough, is it a household pet?"

She pauses near me, arms behind her back. "I have seen him around, I don't know if he is allowed indoors."

I stare at the cat. The cat stares at me.

"What's his name?"

Natalia gives the barest scoff under her breath, as if she can't believe her highly-trained self has been stuck with me. "It is Bad Cat."

"That's a terrible name," I tell the cat. He continues to glare at me until I get up from the bench swing and he takes my place.

I'm back with a tin of salmon I procured from the cook, Natalia still bitterly trailing me. Bad Cat consumes the fish within seconds, then sneers at me as he cleans his face. "I'll see you tomorrow, Bad Cat."

I'm going to make that cat like me. I was never allowed to have a pet as a child. I was foolish enough to try to hide a bluebird once who'd fallen out of the tree, lining the box with cotton and feeding her with an eyedropper. When the maids told my father, he...

Shuddering, I push the memory away. *He can't hurt me. Not anymore. I'm safe.*

I hope.

CHAPTER THIRTEEN

In which Morana is introduced to phone sex.

Cameron...

I've been craving my wife.

First I had to handle a 'mysterious' fire at our bar downtown that leveled one of our most lucrative properties, and then two other jobs that required me to fly to Morocco the next day. They have kept me from her for nearly a week, and it's infuriating.

I suspect that Cormac is sending me off on tasks that someone else could have handled just to fuck with me. He still doesn't trust Morana, and I wonder if he's trying to keep us apart so I don't 'soften' toward her.

Soften. Not likely when all I can think of is her.

It's dusk in the old city of Marrakech. I finished a blistering workout; had a shower and I'm lounging in my sweatpants. My cock's never been harder and I have nowhere to put it. Before getting married, it would have taken thirty minutes at a bar to find a pretty lass, but even if I didn't believe in monogamy, the thought of fucking anyone but Morana makes me itch.

Sitting on my deck at the Royal Mansour Marrakech, I watch the city light up against the spreading darkness and think that having Morana sitting next to me would be the one thing that would make the night perfect.

"Goddamnit, maybe Cormac's right to question me," I groan, rubbing my eyes. Still... I dial Miss Kevin's number.

"Master MacTavish, hello, sir. How may I serve you?"

"Please get one of the secure phones from my office and program it with yours, mine, and Hamish's number and give it to my wife," I say, feeling a surge of anticipation. "Tell her I'll be calling her in ten minutes."

"I would be delighted, sir!" Miss Kevin says happily, making my eyes narrow. I know she's partial to Morana, but she's been making her bias even more obvious.

Pushing down on my swelling cock, I Facetime my wife.

"You gave me a phone!"

"I did. How are you?"

Her smile wavers for a moment and then it's firmly back in place. "Everything is fine here. How are you?"

She's beautiful, sitting on her bed with a t-shirt slipping off one shoulder and her long blonde hair piled up on top of her head. "I'm thinking about you," I admit.

Her smile is sweet and surprised, "Really? In the middle of all those mysterious... *things* you're doing?"

"Even so. Have you been to Marrakech?"

"No! I've always wanted to go there, Morocco's so beautiful." She smiles wistfully.

"I'll bring you with me next time." The words are out of my mouth before I can stop them, but seeing her face light up makes it impossible to regret it. "If it's safe," I amend.

Turning the camera, I pan slowly so she can see the beauty of the city coming alive at night, the flickering lights in a thousand windows like colorful fireflies. "If you were here, I'd take you through the central market, and get you *Halwa Chebakia* cookies for your sweet tooth. I'd buy you silk scarves and drape them all over you until I brought you back to the hotel. Then, I'd use them to tie you to the bed."

I flip the camera in time to see her wide eyes, but she can't fool me. She's not shocked, she's turned on, her violet eyes darken almost to purple when she's close to coming. We've only had one night together, but I remember it vividly.

"The last silk scarf would be used to blindfold you," I continue, rubbing my painfully swelling cock.

She catches the movement. "What are you doing?"

"I'm strokin' myself because you're not here, lass," I growl. "Do you want me to continue the story?"

"Yes?"

"You don't sound certain."

"I am." She flushes an adorable pink and it just makes my dick harder. "Please do."

"Show me what you're wearing," I challenge her. I have to stifle a groan when she shows me the silk shorts she has on, her smooth belly showing as her t-shirt rides up. "If you're wearin' those tiny shorts outside your bedroom, I'll be spanking you purple."

"You're not here to spank me," she says with a saucy little smile I want to kiss off her face.

"Once I blindfold you, I'm going to suck on your nipples, kiss and bite them," I continue, "bite them just a wee bit harder than you can stand, then suck them better and make you beg me to bite them again." Her breath is coming faster, her gaze never leaving me.

"Touch yourself, wife. Put your fingers under your shorts and play with that pretty little pussy." I wait, stroking my cock until her free hand slides slowly under her waistband.

"You can't see me," I continue, "the only thing you can use is how you feel, what you hear. I'll push your thighs wider, tighten the scarves so you can't move an inch. Then I'll play with that sweet-as-sugar cunt with my mouth and fingers. You'll be surprised how far my fingers can reach inside you while I'm sucking on your clit."

Her grip on her phone is a wee shaky, and my gaze drops to her moving hand, still hidden by the silk shorts. "Take those off."

"Not- not this time, okay?" she whispers.

"This time," I agree reluctantly. I want to see what those nimble fingers of hers are up to. Gripping my cock harder, I suck in a breath, forcing myself to slow down. "After you can handle two fingers inside you, I'll add another, and then draw all that silky wet down to your little pucker."

Morana's eyes are wide again. "What?"

"Yes, darlin' did you think I would only be satisfied by your cunt? It's a delicious one, that's certain. So snug and hot…" Groaning, I have to grip myself again. Just looking at this woman is enough to set me off, but she's coming first. "Don't worry. I'll put just one finger in the first time, all wet from your slick, push it inside you while I'm fucking you with my fingers. My lips will be on yours because that should be about the time you'll come for me and I'll smother your screams with my tongue in your mouth. Can you feel it, *mo fhlùr?* You want to come, don't you?"

"Yes…" Her gaze is fixed on mine and with her flushed cheeks and those purple eyes, she has never been more beautiful.

"Do it now. Be my good girl and come. Now!"

She jumps as my tone changes to sharp and demanding, and she does, with a hoarse cry, her back arched and eyes drooping and it sends me into my own, come pouring over my hand as my head drops back.

We sit in silence for a moment, hearing our harsh breaths until she slowly sits up, pushing her hair back.

"Lass, you are the prettiest thing when you come." Laughing when she moans and hides her face, I say, "I'm sorry I canna tidy you up. Take a bath and relax before you go to bed, yeah?"

Clearing her throat awkwardly, Morana nods. "I will. Thank you. I- I mean, it was nice to talk to you, and…"

Chuckling lightly, I rescue her. "It was very nice to talk to you, wife."

"Will you be home soon?" I can tell it costs her to ask this.

"Aye, tomorrow, hopefully. If everything goes to plan."

"All right," she smiles. It's soft, and hopeful and it makes my heart twinge a bit. "I'll see you tomorrow, then. And I want to start our self-defense lessons again!"

"We will," I say, trying to will down my cock, already perkin' up at the thought of wrestling with her. "Goodnight, wife."

"Goodnight, husband."

Ending the call and cleaning myself up, I watch the lights of the city for another hour. Morana still has a role to play before finally being rid of her father, and I'm fighting the guilt that surges up when I think of it.

CHAPTER FOURTEEN

In which we meet the most terrifying mother-in-law in the United Kingdom.

Morana...

It's Day Eight of Operation Bad Cat and he's finally on my lap, purring his croaky, rusty purr as I stroke over his matted fur. I'm sitting on the swing in the garden, feeling his warmth on my lap and wondering if this was how my mother felt.

Bored.

I don't have many pictures of her, my father took them all down. But Valentina, my nanny had found some old photos of my mother and put them into a little album for me. I used to look at them and wonder what she was doing when that picture was taken. Working in the garden? Reading in our library? Hiding from my father?

The life of a Bratva wife is typically a dismal one. Parties, overseeing a household that already had a housekeeper, a cook, and an army of maids. Shopping. I like to believe that my mother and I would have been close, that we would have spent time together, and I could make her proud of me.

While I don't know much about the roles of wives in the Scottish Mafia, I hope they're more interesting than mine. I got the sense that Mala played a more important role in clan business. Without any further word from Cameron about returning to finish my degree, I'm rudderless. There's nowhere I can go, no one to talk to, aside from Miss Kevin who has a full life outside of entertaining my bored self.

When she gave me that phone last night, there were only three numbers programmed in it; hers, Hamish's, and my husband's. My face warms up as I think about our conversation last night. Phone sex was an abrupt escalation in our relationship, but it felt like another building block was placed on our shaky foundation.

I wonder if I could get Mala's number?

Bad Cat digs his claws into me to indicate that he wants off my lap and then leaps free, streaking back under the lavender bush.

Miss Kevin is speed-walking down the path from the house. "Madame MacTavish? The Lady MacTavish is here to see you."

"Do you mean Mala?"

"No." Her face is pale, who could possibly be scary enough to alarm our implacable butler? "Lady Elspeth MacTavish."

"You mean, Cameron's mother?" I ask hoarsely.

"Indeed, please come with me."

Wiping cat hair off my black skirt as fast as I can, I head up the path at a near-gallop to keep up with her. "Tell me what I need to know!" I gasp, "How do I address her? Is she scary? She's terrifying, isn't she? You look like you're about to wet yourself and you're the head of staff for an organized crime kingpin!"

We're at the kitchen door and she spins, smoothing my hair. I'm wondering if she's going to wet her thumb with her spit and clear a smudge off my cheek.

"Address her as Lady MacTavish until invited to address her otherwise. Smile, but don't smile too much, she hates people toadying up to her. You're the wife of a MacTavish, so straighten your shoulders and remember it!" The kindly, calm Miss Kevin has been replaced by a wide-eyed doppelganger who sounds like she's sending me into battle.

If possible, I'm more terrified now.

Lady Elspeth MacTavish is seated in the drawing room, though I didn't know it was called that and have passed it maybe once. There is a full tea set in front of her with macarons and little sandwiches.

Wiping my sweaty hands on my skirt, I smile, trying to remember not to make it too wide. "Lady MacTavish, it's a pleasure- honor- it's lovely to meet you. I'm-"

"The young lady my son married in a wedding dress meant for another groom by our rather displeased family priest," she interrupts, looking me over thoroughly. After a painfully long moment, she nods to the couch. "Do have a seat."

Elspeth MacTavish is a smaller woman, slender, elegant in a blue Yves Saint Laurent suit and silvered blonde hair. Cameron has her perfectly sculpted nose and jawline, though his height clearly comes from his father.

"In all fairness, none of that was my plan, ma'am," I say, smoothing my skirt over my knees and finding more cat hair.

To my shock, she chuckles lightly. "Yes, that would be Cameron, the boy never stood on ceremony."

Smiling uneasily, I wait as she assumes the role of hostess and makes me a cup of tea. "So, how are you settling in?"

"Miss Kevin has been very kind and helpful," I flounder a bit. "Cameron is busy in Morocco as we speak, but I'm hoping he'll be home tonight."

Why isn't that evil prick here now instead of leaving me alone with his mother?

She eyes me over her teacup. "You sound surprisingly warm when you speak of my son, given the origins of your relationship."

"Well, it comes and goes," I admit without thinking.

This makes her laugh, even if she looks a little surprised

that she's amused. "My second-born can be infuriating upon occasion, but he has a good heart and he is very loyal to those who are loyal to him."

"Can you tell me why he hates my father's Bratva so much?" I ask, circling the teacup on the plate. "It has to be a horrible thing to risk so much."

"That, I will not say. You will have to get the story from Cameron."

"He won't tell me," I say despondently.

"Then you'll have to continue asking him." She's crisp and getting on the chilly side, so I hastily change the subject.

At the end of an excruciating hour of being interrogated about everything from my education to my immunizations, she rises. "Walk me to the door."

"Of course, Lady MacTavish."

Her bodyguard opens the door for her as she settles her purse on her arm. "We'll be having Sunday dinner at the estate. The rest of the family is understandably curious about you. I will tell them all to be on their best behavior. None of them will be."

I bite back a smile. "I understand. Thank you, ma'am."

She looks me over one last time, her head slightly cocked. "You did not get your father's looks."

"No," I say fervently. "I'm told I resemble my mother."

"That is fortunate." Her eyes move to the elaborate koi pond in front of the house. "What happened to the koi? They were quite rare and exotic creatures."

My gaze follows hers to see all of Cameron's wildly expensive fish, floating belly-up in the pond. He loves feeding those little guys, I'd seen him out there every evening.

Oh, my god, I think, feeling horrible. *The Curse of the Ivanov's has made me a goldfish murderess.*

Lady Elspeth gives the poor fish corpses one more disapproving look. "Well, goodbye."

I stand on the wide granite steps, waving goodbye politely and as her car turns onto the street, I abruptly sit down. She is terrifying. A tiny, terrifying tornado of a woman.

It is not five minutes later that the gate opens again and Cameron gets out of one of the Range Rovers.

"A nice welcome, wife, though not expected," he grins, his lecherous gaze moving up and down my body.

"It's not for *you*, your mother just left."

His eyes widened. "Ma was here? I'll be damned. How did it go?"

"It would have gone better if you had been here!" I want to smack his arm but we're still outside and I don't know if that's against the rules for my crime lord husband's image. "She told me that we're coming to Sunday dinner at the estate, that - and I quote - 'the rest of the family wants to get a look at me.'"

Sliding an arm around my waist, he pulls me inside the house. "Well, you passed my mother's test. Everyone else will fall into line. I'm impressed, wife."

"How did I pass her test?"

"She's like a cat, she must come to you. I couldn't introduce you to the rest of the family until she invited you. She approves of you." His arm has slipped down a bit and his hand is almost resting on my ass.

Looking back briefly at the tragedy in the koi pond, I allow him to lead me into the house. I'll tell him later. "Is there a reason you're attempting to molest me in the hallway?"

"You're right," he agrees, "I won't molest you in the hallway. The library, on the other hand..."

Sweeping me up as I give a startled yelp, Cameron takes off for the library.

CHAPTER FIFTEEN

In which Morana's past rises up to haunt her.

Morana...

When my phone rings, I nearly leap across the table to get it. There are only three people who have my number, and Hamish and Miss Kevin are here.

"Hello, husband. Please tell me there are no more mysterious trips to Morocco?"

"How sweet, Morana Ivanova. So nice to see you've settled into your Stockholm Syndrome so easily."

I swallow past a surge of nausea. "How did you get my number, Artim Ivanov?"

"Did you think your father would give up on you that easily? Or Vadik Stepanov? He executed twenty-eight guards that day." His oily voice makes me feel dirty, coated with his shared filth. I look around the deck wildly, as if expecting him to step out of the bushes.

"You're going to have to find something else to sell off for the Bratva, Artim Ivanov. I'm married, and no longer useful as collateral." There's sweat beading on my forehead but I'm shivering.

He's disgusted. "You are happy believing you are married to that *kusok der'ma,* that piece of shit?"

"Cameron doesn't beat me up and rape me in front of his men, so that seems a positive beginning," I say.

"What do you really think he wants you for, cousin? Do you think his family will welcome a daughter from the Bratva that killed his second? A member of their clan?"

Sitting down abruptly, I ask, "What are you talking about?"

"He didn't tell you? But I thought there was such trust between you," he sneers.

"I'm hanging up."

"Wait! Morana Ivanova, you must listen to me." The desperation in his voice makes me pause. I hate him. But I've never heard him sound this way.

"Our Bratva killed his second in command, Ferr MacTavish, when we caught him spying, along with some of his men. He was their cousin. Cameron took you as revenge. Our sources say he's bragging about fooling you into thinking you're married. He's ruined you and laughs about it."

I don't believe him. Artim is a bastard. He's a liar...

"You don't need to worry. The Pakhan has no intention of stealing you back," he says, suddenly sounding exhausted. "The Stepanov Bratva is cutting ties with us unless we pay a fee for Vadik's lost bride. Now that you're spoiled, he doesn't want you, either."

"Then there's nothing left to say, I'm hanging up."

"Morana Ivanova, you may hate us all, but when the MacTavish bastards dump you in the street, you will have nothing. Help us, and we will help you." There's a pleading, desperate tone I've never heard from Artim before. Is it really that dire?

"What do you want, Artim Ivanov? You know I don't have any money."

"We know you don't. What you do have is your tracking chip."

My blood turns to ice. How could I have been so stupid? Everyone in my father's Bratva has a tracking chip inserted under the skin on their shoulder. They've known exactly where I am, likely right down to the square foot this entire time. "So that was you, trying to break into the house that night."

"We wanted to find you and scan the chip, that was all," he protested. "We tried to find you at the fundraiser but we didn't get there in time."

"So, you've been tracking me since I left Moscow," I say numbly.

"Since he kidnapped you from your own wedding, cousin!"

Pinching the bridge of my nose against an oncoming headache, I wish I'd never picked up. "What exactly do you need from my chip, Artim Ivanov?"

"Your father inserted the bank codes for his offshore interests in your chip," he says, sounding troublingly sincere. "It's the last place anyone would think to look for them."

I chuckle mirthlessly, "Because who would trust a mere woman with anything sensitive, correct?"

"It will take me five seconds to scan your chip and download the codes," he says wearily. "After that, you can deactivate or remove the chip. We will not contact you again, if that's your wish. But your father gives his word that he will set up a bank account that only you can access. You'll have a... what do they call it? A nest egg if you need it. You can disappear."

"Why should I trust anything you say?" I demand, my throat's closing up, and the chills are back.

There's a short silence, and Artim says, "Marriage records, whether civil or religious are listed in the city records in Edinburgh. You can look them up online. You've been 'married' for over two weeks. Go look for yourself."

I hate the way he mockingly says *married*. I hate that part of me still wonders if it's all part of Cameron's plan. I especially hate that I am going to look it up the moment I'm off this call.

"Search the records, cousin," he says, with a tone that almost sounds like pity. I want to reach through the phone and claw his vocal cords out for having the nerve to sound that way. "I will call you tonight at 7pm, Morana Ivanova. This is your chance as well as ours."

Staring at the silent phone in my hand, I feel all the shame of my childhood rising up again. The misfortune I was told that I brought to my family. That I was an ill wind. I don't owe those bastards anything. I don't.

The hallway is quiet in the main part of the house, I hear Miss Kevin's gentle voice instructing one of the maids in the library. My phone doesn't have internet access, but I know where to find it. The butler's office is next to the kitchen, a tidy little space where I've shared tea with Miss Kevin once or twice. I know that she always keeps her phone on her, but her laptop is usually open.

My shaking fingers make it hard to type quickly and I keep glancing up at the doorway. Edinburgh's online records are surprisingly organized, and it takes just a few keystrokes to look for our names.

They're not in the marriage records.

I check a couple of other places in the files. Cormac and Mala's marriage is proudly recorded, nothing for Cameron and me. I type our names into the search bar just to see if anything comes up, and there's one short blurb from a local gossip site mentioning we were seen together at the Gala. Nothing about us being married.

But his mother... She invited us to dinner? She told me that I'd be meeting the rest of the family. Was her visit just part of his game to sell the story?

Hearing soft footsteps, I hastily exit out of the site and escape Miss Kevin's office just in time.

"Hello, Madame MacTavish, can I get you anything?"

She always smiles so kindly at me. Is that part of the game too, just to keep me complacent?

"Are you all right?" Her head's cocked, looking at me quizzically and I realize I'm standing in front of the open freezer door.

"Oh… I'm sorry, I was just looking for… Ice cream." I grab the closest pint and hold it up. "I'll get a spoon and eat it out on the deck."

There's a fierce wind blowing outside today, but she nods politely, heading down the little hall to her office.

Cameron is still out on whatever business he has tonight of making deals or breaking legs, as I sit on my bed, staring at my phone. When it rings right at 7pm, I want to throw it out the window. Answering it will prove that Artim is right.

"*Privet,* Artim Ivanov."

"*Privet,* hello, Morana Ivanova." He sounds tired, like he hasn't slept in days.

Good.

"MacTavish is taking you to an event tomorrow night, as I'm sure he's told you." There's his old malice coming back.

"Go on," I say, rubbing my eyes, which are suspiciously damp.

"It's the opening night of their newest club. He will keep you in the VIP section, of course. There is a private bathroom on that level. Meet me there at 10pm exactly."

"And you will do what, Artim Ivanov? I don't trust you. What would stop you from kidnapping me?"

He sighs, "You will be in the middle of a MacTavish club with bulletproof security. Even if you wanted me to, there's no way I could get you out of there. I will scan your chip and upload the information. It takes a matter of seconds. Then, I can disable the chip for you if you wish it. We will send you a notification of your bank information within the week."

"I don't want anything from the Ivanov Bratva," I say numbly. "Just take the codes and go."

"You'll be there, Morana Ivanova?"

Looking around my lonely bedroom, I shrug. "I'll be there."

CHAPTER SIXTEEN

In which we are introduced to the immortal phrase, "Ya' finger licking shit monkey."

Morana...

I don't see Cameron until the next day, when he creeps into my bedroom, waking me up with slow kisses down my neck.

"Good morning, wife," he murmurs, heading lower toward my breasts.

Grabbing his hair to halt his progress, I make him look at me. "A little presumptuous, *husband*."

He chuckled, sitting up. "Aye, you've not seen hide nor hair of me for a day and a half, have ye'? I'm sorry. This new club has been a bear to open."

I'm still puzzling over what a bear would have to do with it when he starts those diabolical kisses again. "Stop! What's- what's this about a club?"

"Aye, I'll be taking you there tonight for the grand opening. Pick something sexy to wear. Not too sexy!" His gaze goes down the length of me, still in bed and clutching a pillow to my chest. "Something with a high neck. And long."

Laughing a little, I try to ignore the ache in my chest. "I'll see what I can find."

"How many clubs and bars does your family own?"

We're heading into the New Town section of Edinburgh, where

the latest MacTavish club is opening on George Street.

"Twenty-eight," Cameron says, intent on his texting. "Along with thirty restaurants, a handful of spas… they're excellent for laundering money. Most are in Glasgow and London, a couple in Paris. *Gnìomhan Dorcha* is our biggest one thus far."

"*Gnìomhan Dorcha?*"

Now he looks up, a slow smile spreading over his face as he touches my nearly bare thigh. "Club Dark Deeds."

Moving my leg away, I look out the window again. "Seems fitting."

If my chilliness offends him, Cameron doesn't say anything about it. Smiling rakishly, he says, "There'll be a lot of media there tonight, we have most of the players from the Celtic F.C. coming in. Smile and show off your pretty ring, darlin' and I'll show off my pretty wife."

Forcing a smile, I remind myself that he's just like the others. Everyone wants something from me. He's not any different.

A flurry of shouts rises from the long line of people waiting to get in as we exit the SUV. As we pass the main entrance, the steel security fence breaks in two places and there's a melee as the crowd tries to take advantage of it. I see Hamish urgently speaking into a headset and three of the security men racing to contain the breach.

"How the hell did that happen?" Cameron snaps at Hamish, who looks bewildered.

"I dinna' know," Hamish says, "all the security fencing was double-checked this afternoon."

Just my version of malicious workplace compliance, I think. *You wanted me. You get all my catastrophic karmic baggage too.*

Smoothing down my glittering black dress, I notice I'm likely the most covered up of any woman here, though there's a long slit up the side of my skirt. I picked a dress that left my shoulders bare to make it easy for...

What am I doing?

I'm really going to throw myself into the mouth of the dragon? I could tell Cameron that my horrible cousin is here tonight. He could take him and that would be one less threat from the Ivanov Bratva.

He's not your husband. You don't owe him anything.

Tomorrow, I'll suddenly 'remember' that I have this chip stuck in my shoulder and ask to get it removed. Then when no one has a way to track me, I'll disappear.

Club Dark Deeds lives up to its name, the dance floor soars up three stories and the space above it is filled with nets and long lines of silks. Aerial performers spin and dive over the crowds and dazzling rainbows of light play over the walls and multiple bars. The crowd is six deep at each bar as the men and women there race back and forth to fetch drinks. They're dressed as devils and angels, there's a few demons serving drinks in the crowd and some fairies dancing on top of tables around the perimeter, their glittering wings happily flapping with their movements.

Cameron is taking me through the crowd, a possessive arm around my waist and I almost trip over my high heels as I try to take it all in.

"This is incredible!" I say, stumbling against him.

"I'm glad you're enjoyin' it," he says, giving me a quick, careless kiss that makes my heart ache. "I'm taking you up to the VIP section, you'll have a view of everything from there."

We rise in a glass elevator, and I put my feet together when I realize the floor is transparent, too. "What do we call this, double duty lift *and* upskirt view?"

He frowns as he looks down to see several eyes gazing up. "You are correct, wife. That will be taken care of immediately."

"It's nice to know I'm good for something." I don't hide my bitterness well enough and I see him frown before turning to look out over the crowd.

"Morana! What do you think?"

Mala's heading for me with a huge grin. She leans in as if she intends to give me the traditional Russian three-kiss greeting, but pulls back when she sees my shoulders curl in. I can't bear her fake warmth. I feel foolish enough thinking that any of these people wanted me here.

"It's... something," I agree. One of the shirtless male aerial performers swinging next to the balcony winks at me.

"Come sit down, darlin' I'll walk you around on a little tour in a moment." Cameron leads me over to a sectional, a butter-soft blue suede that's surrounded by beautiful little chandeliers dripping with colorful crystals. They give the feeling of being enclosed within them, an illusion of intimacy.

The illusion. That's something I can relate to.

"How have you been?" Mala asks, handing me a glass of champagne. She's wearing a gorgeous red dress with a beaded halter top and Cormac is hovering over her protectively. "I was so excited to see you tonight. I don't get out much with our twins being the wild animals they are. Something they picked up from their father."

She laughs as he leans down to kiss her, and my heart hurts. The connection between these two is palpable. I can feel the love they have for each other. I'd allowed myself the slightest hope that maybe I could build that with Cameron. I'm a fool. I put on my bright social smile and listen to her complain good-naturedly about how much candy Catriona and Michael get from their uncles.

"It sounds like you are not to be trusted," I smile sweetly at

Cameron. He smiles back, but for one moment, his eyes are sad.

The men leave for a while to keep an eye on the opening and shake a few hands. "Don't you need to be mingling, too?" I ask. "You're the queen of the clan, aren't you?"

"Oh, god don't say it like that!" Mala shudders. "I'm American. That all sounds so weird to me. Sometimes, I have to be with Cormac and make the rounds, but he spares me whenever he can. Now, how are you settling in? I heard you got the royal invitation to Sunday dinner."

"Are Cameron's parents officially a Lord and a Lady?"

"They are," she nods, "but even if they weren't, we'd still call Elspeth that. She's definitely more suited as Queen of the MacTavish Clan than I am."

It's 9:55. Draining another glass of champagne, I stand, looking for the hall for the bathrooms.

"Oh, do you need the ladies' room?" Mala stands, too. "There's a private one for the owners, I'll show you if you-"

"No need," I cut her off with a tight smile, "but thanks."

As soon as I head in the right direction, I groan. Natalia, my unfriendly shadow is right behind me. I don't know how I'm going to pull this off. She opens the bathroom door, checks inside quickly, and moves aside for me. When I move to close the door, she puts a foot in the way.

"I've got it from here, thanks," I raise an eyebrow, "or do you just want to make sure I wipe?"

As expected, her face scrunches in disgust and she steps back.

Shutting the door with a sigh, I look around. It's empty.

There's a knock on the door, and I roll my eyes, opening it. "Natalia, give me a-"

Artim grabs me by the arm, sticking his pistol in my ribs, half-hidden by his jacket. My bodyguard is between two other men, a gun jammed in the small of her back. "*Svoloch'*, you bastard!" I hiss, "Of course, you'd be a lying piece of garbage."

"*Zakroy svoy shlyukhovyy rot,* shut your whore mouth," he snarls, grabbing a fistful of my hair with his other hand and yanking it until I can feel some strands tearing loose. "Did you really think we would let you prance off? If you don't want to be the Pakhan's wife, you can be his whore."

He tries pulling me along and I dig in my heels. "I would rather have you shoot me than go back with you. So just do it." The hall is eerily quiet for such a busy night and I wonder if he's got men blocking the entrance. There's no help coming.

"Fine," he rasps, "then I'll shoot your useless bodyguard bitch. She didn't even see us coming."

One of the other men cocks his gun.

"Wait!" My voice is shaking and I despise myself for being so stupid. "Wait. I'll go with you. Just leave her here. Don't hurt her."

Nearly yanking my arm out of the socket, Artim drags me down the hallway to another flight of stairs, they're narrow and scuffed, this must be a service entrance. The stairs feel loose and slippery and I stumble once, hauled up again by my cursing cousin.

He's not shoving the gun as hard into my side, trying to keep his balance, too. As we get to the bottom, Cameron and Dougal step out and Cameron slams his Glock into Artim's head, sending him to his knees as he kicks the gun away from him. There's a grunt and a thud behind me, and Cameron's arm loops around my waist, swinging me out of the way as one of the Ivanov men falls down the stairs, dead. The other now has Natalia's gun pressed under his chin, forcing his head back.

"Welcome to Scotland, ya' finger-licking shit monkey," Dougal says pleasantly, kicking Artim in the ribs.

CHAPTER SEVENTEEN

In which Cameron admits this might have been a mistake.

Cameron...

Morana's staring at me, pale-faced and her lips pressed together. If I had been expecting a tearful display of gratitude for saving her, I'd be mighty disappointed. But my wife is a smart girl, she's already figured it out.

"You used me as bait."

I nod to my men and they haul her cousin and his minions off, struggling and cursing the entire way. She doesn't take her gaze off me.

We're standing in the hallway that's just off the kitchen, and there's the faint sounds of pots clanging and chatter from the chef and his crew. My remaining men and Natalia stand silently, waiting for an order. Sparing them a glance, I say, "Excuse us."

They leave us alone.

My bride is slight and delicate with her high cheekbones, lean arms and legs. Her heels raise her up several inches, but I prefer her barefoot when she comes just to my shoulder and I can pick her up easily and...

Fecking focus, mate.

She's slight, but she's strong. While she may not be crying, her eyes have a slight glossiness and her chin is up, like a Tsarina, fists clenched.

"Didn't you?"

"Yes," I answer honestly.

"He could have killed Natalia. He was going to."

I notice she doesn't mention the threat to herself. "You were never in any danger, we had him surrounded from the second he-"

She slaps me.

It's a solid, respectable blow. Walking away, she pauses, turning in a disoriented circle. "I don't know where to go."

My wife's voice is flat, emotionless and her blank, Bratva princess demeanor takes over. I'd seen her about a year ago, when we were doing some surveillance on the Ivanov Bratva. She was back in Moscow for a short break from school, and in the forty-eight hours we watched the house and the comings and goings, she never deviated from this expression.

I hold out my hand. "This way."

She steps away from me, walking in the right direction, a frigid wall between us that feels as real as a block of ice. Hamish and two bodyguards fall in behind her, heading for the SUV waiting in the VIP parking lot.

"I'm not sure how you're going to sweet-talk your way out of this," Dougal says. "She looks dead inside, that one."

"It had to be this way." I'm still watching my wife walk away, her back straight, never looking back. "We couldn't risk her raising any suspicion. You'll note that she also never told me about his call."

He shrugged, "Why would she? She knew you didn't trust her either."

There's a crash of tearing metal and broken glass, and we charge out the door with our guns drawn to see a terrified valet tumbling out of the Porsche that he just rear-ended into the Range Rover.

That my wife had been about to enter.

"What the feckin' hell? You're fired, you feckin'-" I've got a grip on the valet's red jacket and I'm shaking him like a terrier with a rat and then Morana begins to laugh. She laughs and laughs, ignoring me and brushing off anyone's attempt to touch her until Hamish brings around another SUV.

"How is your lovely bride?"

Rubbing my eyes, I growl, "About as good as ya' can expect."

"So, complete shite, then." Cormac's tone is not unsympathetic.

After listening through both conversations Morana had with Artim, that cock-sucking donkey fucker, it was clear she had no intention of betraying us. Knowing how they had treated her all her life, I don't understand why she would risk getting near any of them again. Maybe she was simply naive enough to hope that if she did as they asked, the Ivanovs would finally leave her alone.

Her cousin's such a stupid shite that it never occurred to him to be suspicious about how easily he intercepted the cell signal from Morana's phone and got the number. He thought he was pulling off some real undercover fuckery.

"I quizzed Nikandr again about what he thought he saw at the auction that night, as you asked," Cormac says. Now, his tone is faintly apologetic. "After running through some of the surveillance video from the auction, he says the woman was another cousin. It was Artim's sister, not Morana."

"This is information that would have been much more helpful WEEKS AGO!" I shout. "Goddamnit, I treated her like shite!"

"Apparently, the cousin looks a great deal like her, the same blonde hair, similar build," he continued as if I wasn't shouting at him.

"She feckin' hates me," I say, running a hand through my hair. "I promised her I'd take her to Morocco." There's a quizzical silence from Cormac, but I'm hit with the enormity of how this must feel for Morana. I've used my wife. Just like everyone else in her life.

"Brother, I'm thinking you care more about her than you expected to," he ventures.

"I can't fix this."

"Aye, you can. Women are not as complex as you think. Don't fuck anyone else. Keep your word. Be honest about the things you want. Tell her that you will fulfill these three things and she'll forgive you." Cormac hums thoughtfully. "Though if my wife were in the room, she would likely add that Morana will and should make you suffer first."

"Thank you. Your words of wisdom are profound," I say sourly.

"You're welcome," he says pleasantly. "When you do get Morana to speak to you again, tell her that Mala would like to take her out to lunch. Are you two coming to Ma's Sunday dinner tomorrow?"

"Not unless I can get her to leave her room."

Morana...

The doctor came today and removed the tracker from my shoulder, leaving a small incision. "This will heal quickly," he says kindly, "just keep it clean."

It was the only thing I'd asked Miss Kevin for last night before I walked up to my room and locked the door. I can't look at anyone. They all knew. She left a breakfast tray outside the door when I wouldn't answer her repeated knocking and polite inquiry. Same with lunch. The sun is setting, sending long shadows over the back garden and I see Bad Cat, sitting on his swing.

Bad Cat used me too, for cans of salmon. But at least he was honest about his intentions.

There's another knock on the door, heavier this time, impatient. "Morana, open up."

Fucking Cameron.

The pounding on the door increases. "I just want to talk, open the door and- fecking hell!"

Fucking Cameron's fist has punched right through what I thought was a very solid oak door, and when he tries to pull his hand out of the hole he's made, a jagged shard of wood tears a cut along his forearm.

Smiling, I go into the bathroom and lock that door.

CHAPTER EIGHTEEN

In which we address Fucking Cameron and his box of murder things.

Cameron...

"Tell me."

After two days of nothing from Morana's room, I'm reduced to daily reports from Miss Kevin regarding my wife's doings. Every part of me wants to kick open her door and force her to listen to me. Except for my last clump of common sense, which is telling me that to do that will be to lose her forever.

Miss Kevin folds her hands in front of her. "Her bedroom door was replaced yesterday. Today, she finally had breakfast. She also asked me for a litter box."

"A litter box? Why the hell- shite. She's found Bad Cat, hasn't she? Did you tell her that mangy thing is not an indoor pet?"

"No," she says politely, "I have said no such thing."

"Why not?"

"Because I believe she will not open her door again if I attempt to challenge her on small issues."

"So, she has the cat and she ate breakfast," I rub my eyes. "Anything else?"

"Madame MacTavish also requested a tin of salmon."

"This is all very fascinating," I say impatiently. "Anything else? How does she look?"

"She won't look at me," Miss Kevin sounds a bit sad. "But your wife looks exactly the way she did when she came home that night from the club, if that is of any use."

It's as if she wants to make me feel worse.

"Thank you for the report."

We've moved that rat bastard Artim around a couple of times to discourage any thought of a rescue attempt by Anatoly Ivanov, but I suspect there won't be one. Thanks to our attacks on his trucking company that's used to transport human souls for the Stepanov Bratva, he's got bigger issues.

"Hey, motherfucker. Good mornin'!"

I kick the side of Artim's cot, knocking him off and onto the floor.

"You look like shite, my friend. Late night?"

He curls up on the concrete floor, moaning. "Just kill me and get it over with."

"Well, now you're making me look like a bad host," I say, nudging him over on his back with the toe of my boot. I pull up a chair and seat myself. "Let's have a chat about your bratva's interests in St. Petersburg. You're not supposed to be messing about in the Morozov and Turgenev territory, are ya' now?"

After another hour with my boots and fists and the occasional lashing of a heavy length of chain, I have what I need from him. It all confirms what Nolan O'Rourke told us.

"I'd give you a long farewell speech, but ya' deserve nothing," I say, pulling out my Glock. His eyes are both nearly swollen shut, so I'm not sure if he sees it. But he twitches when I release the safety. "If I were feelin' all sentimental about it, I'd burn you alive, the way you did Ferr. You're not worth the trouble. So, for Ferr. And for Morana."

I shoot him.

Watching his bloodied body go slack, I ponder that anyone who says revenge is a dish best served cold has never shot an arsehole like this in the face.

Morana...

The sun rises and sets again, and I don't want to leave the chair by my window. Bad Cat seems all right about staying in my room with me, so we watch people go back and forth, guards making their rounds, gardeners, and occasionally, Miss Kevin who will look up at my windows, shielding her eyes from the sun.

I can't seem to care.

Picking apart all the sticky strands of my humiliation, fury, and disillusionment feels like too much work, so I let them wrap around me, tighter and tighter until I sit, numb in my cocoon.

Eventually, I will be forced to talk to fucking Cameron. I'll ask him how much longer I'll have to stay here, when will my usefulness in his revenge plans end. When can I leave? But for now, I look out the window and pet the heavy warmth of Bad Cat on my lap.

Two days later...

"Wife! Wake the fuck up!"

That idiot is pounding so hard on my door that it's vibrating on the hinges. He's going to break it again. Maybe he'll use his head this time. The vision of fucking Cameron's head wedged helplessly in my door makes me smile for a lovely moment until he kicks the door open.

Bad Cat gives a screech, scratches me, and races for the safety of my closet.

Holding my bleeding hand up to keep from messing up my sheets, I stare at my husband.

It's six in the morning, the sun is barely up.

"It's time to start up your self-defense lessons again," fucking Cameron announces. He dumps a box on the bed, it tips over and an assortment of knives fall out. "Pick a blade, we're going to work on-"

"Take your box of murder things and get the hell out of my room."

He grabs my wrist. "What happened to your hand?"

"You do not touch me! Let go!" I'm pulling and so is he and now blood drops are flying everywhere.

"Stop," he says sternly, holding my hand still. "We have to clean this up." He pulls me toward the bathroom as if I have no idea how to walk on my own. "Cat scratches can get infected easily."

"I wouldn't have been scratched if you hadn't started pounding on the door." His grip is firm around my wrist but he's not hurting me but I would love to hurt *him*. Scratch him, punch him... do something to make him feel the way I do.

Holding my hand under cold water in the sink, he looks up at me in the mirror. "Ya' shouldn't have that beast in the house, he's a feckin' nightmare."

My wet hand clenches into a fist. "If you try to take Bad Cat away from me I will stab you in the throat. That is a promise."

"I thought you told me to take my box of murder things away," he counters, "what will you use?"

"Why are you here?" I hiss, "I don't want to see you. None of this is real." Humiliatingly, my eyes are wet. "Get your fucking revenge, decimate the Ivanovs, and for the love of god, let me go!"

Fucking Cameron carefully dries off my hand and pulls a first aid box out from under the sink.

"I can do it!" I try to pull loose from his grip and he ignores me, spraying disinfectant on the bleeding scratch and covering it with a band aid. Now I can feel the sting from the cut and it hits me, how numb I've been.

"It's clear a conversation is overdue," he finally says, lifting his head to look at me. Without ceremony, he hoists me up on the bathroom counter so I'm looking at him, eye to eye. "I know what happened at the club hurt you. You must feel betrayed. I won't apologize for it. That had to happen. Your fuckface cousin gave us corroboration for some very important information about the Red Trade. Your father jumped into the Stepanov business with both feet."

I want to look away from him because I really hate him so much, but he's speaking to me. Honestly, directly. "This isn't all about revenge for me, lass."

"It is," I say. "I know about your cousin. I know Artim killed him."

"Artim didn't just kill Ferr. He burned him alive, along with ten of our men. He broke into an Ivanov warehouse in Moscow too soon, I was meant to meet up with him and bring in my team. The Ivanovs were comin' for the women early, so he broke in and rescued them. Twenty-six girls, most of 'em were under eighteen. Ferr's team got the girls out, but he stayed with some of our men to draw fire and give the others a chance to get away. Artim chained the warehouse shut and set it ablaze." Cameron's expression is oddly blank as he recites this.

"I hope you did the same to him." It bursts out of me, shocking me with the intensity of it.

"He wasn't worth the effort," he says flatly.

He looks down at my scratched hand, smoothing the band-aid down. "Bad Cat is Ferr's cat. I went to his house to get him and the little fecker scratched the hell out of me. He roams around here like he's the king, but he would never come into the house until you brought him in."

Cameron's standing between my legs and suddenly, the heat of his body so close, the scent of him sparks my center again, making me ache. I never knew you could hate someone and still want to fuck them at the same time.

Lesson learned. Because I want him to pull down my sleep shorts and slide into me. I would wrap my legs around that narrow waist of his and…

Not my husband.

Pulling my head back, I watch him in silence as he puts the first aid kit away. "Now that you have what you needed from Artim, will you let me go?"

He has the fucking gall to look puzzled.

"We're married, lass. In case you've forgotten."

All my helplessness and fury surge up and I scream, "Liar!" Shoving him back as hard as I can, I take advantage of his surprise to leap off the counter and race out of the room.

CHAPTER NINETEEN

In which all arguments should be resolved in a heavenly pool house.

Morana...

It's raining, the grass is slippery as I charge through the back gardens. I don't know where I'm going but I won't stay in the house with fucking Cameron.

For a moment, he was being honest with me. He told me about his poor cousin, he told me Artim was dead. I didn't even feel a flicker of remorse. Then he has the fucking audacity to lie to me *again?*

"Wife! Come back in the house!"

The Laird of the Manor is roaring like a bear trampling through the woods and with about as much subtlety. Anyone in the household who was not awake to witness this debacle certainly is now. I see one of his guards walking toward me, he looks over my shoulder and abruptly turns the other way.

Putting on a burst of speed, I round the lavender bush and nearly trip, knocking my hip painfully into the swing under the oak tree and sending it flying.

Right into fucking Cameron.

"Christ, woman!" Skidding to a stop, I watch the blood gush from his nose. "This is the second time you've nearly broken my nose, what the hell do you have against my face?"

"Because it's *yours!*" I shout, "You lying sack of shit! Why do you keep playing with me? I know we're not married!"

He looks at me as if the light has finally dawned.

"You believed Ivanov when he was talkin' shite about the marriage being fake? You'd really believe that son of a bitch over me?"

"He told me to check the city records! We do not have a marriage license! Cormac and Mala's is there, but there is nothing for us!"

He frowns, clearly not picking up on the key points in my statement. "How did you get online?"

"Why does that matter?" I scream, "The point is that you fucking lied to me. Your whole family did and this is so sick!"

"Christ, woman!" He runs his hands through his wet hair, his bloody nose forgotten. "Why is this so important to you?"

"Because now I'm sp-"

Spoiled. I was going to say, "I'm spoiled and no other man will want me." *Bozhe moy*, the indoctrination was that thorough. Part of me has always believed that my virginity was the only thing of value I had to offer.

"What? You're what?" He reaches for me and I slap his hand away. "We are married, for better and for worse, though we're gettin' a lot of the latter part. I haven't lied to you, not once. Yes, I withheld information, but I did not lie."

"Yes, my trust in you has grown by *leaps and bounds* after the night when you used me as bait," I sneer.

"Son of a motherless whore!" he shouts to the sky, "I am sorry, lass. It had to be done. I do ugly things sometimes, dark things. But the women and children your feckin' father is moving around for Stepanov do not deserve what's bein' done to them. We started moving against the Ivanovs before they killed Ferr. Yes, I want to avenge him. But Ferr would tell you there's something more important than revenge. It's rescue.

"So yes, I kidnapped you. I used you to draw in your cousin. This is true. But if you are the woman I believe you are, you would have done both things willingly if it helped those girls."

The rain is pouring down his face, rinsing away the blood and turning his t-shirt transparent against his sculpted chest.

He's right. I didn't know my father was already in the Red Trade with Stepanov. If I had, I would have done anything I could.

Maybe I still have something of value to offer after all.

Surging forward, I kiss him, hard, mouths crashing together and I try to angle the kiss so I'm not bumping his wounded nose again. His fingers are weaving through my wet hair holding me to him, kissing me back greedily.

I'm startled into a shriek when he swings me up in his arms and heads in the opposite direction, moving toward the back of the house. There's a glassed-in building I haven't seen before - do things just pop up out of the ground overnight here?

"What is that?" There's steam inside, condensing on the glass and I can't see inside.

Opening the door with a nudge of his shoulder, he says, "The pool house." It's a smaller pool, a vivid blue with lush plants around it.

"You have a pool house?"

"*We* have a pool house," he corrects and walks right into the deep end. My scream is smothered as we sink under the water and I hastily surface, kicking for the side.

"You asshole! Why did you do that?" I'm angrily pushing my wet hair out of my face as he heads for me with a swift breaststroke.

"We were already wet," he shrugs and kisses me again, blocking me in with an arm on the pool's edge on either side of me. The perverted, conniving bastard has already managed to get his sleep pants off and I can feel his cock, hard and heavy against me. "Tell me you want me."

"You asshole! I hate you!" My nails are digging into his wet shirt, he doesn't seem to notice.

"Keep talking," he laughs, "you're only making me harder." His big hand cups my center, the heat radiating through the thin, wet cloth. "Tell me you want me."

"No. You can't keep- keep grabbing me and dragging me around!"

Cameron's long fingers have managed to slide under my shorts and he's yanking them down. "You have until the count of three to tell me what I want to hear," he threatens.

"Why? What happens on three?"

Sliding two fingers inside me he watches me suck in my breath so fast that I cough. "Something you won't like, wife."

I don't believe him. I think I *will* like it. Pressing my lips together, I narrow my eyes challengingly.

Thrusting a third finger inside me, he grips my pussy hard. The heel of his hand is pushing against my clitoris and the whole thing is so filthy and outrageous that I nearly come. He squeezes me again. Tightly.

"Tell me what I want to hear, *wife*."

"I want you!" I snap, and my heels dig into the small of his back as he fucks me with his fingers, grinding his hand roughly against me. After he makes me come, shaking and moaning, he pulls his hand away and replaces it with his cock.

"Slide down me," he growls in my ear and I push, gasping as I impale myself on his thick cock, bracing my back against the pool wall.

No one should be this big.

I can feel myself stretching open for him, wider than I thought was possible as I work inch after inch inside me. "Pretty, filthy girl, impaled on my cock and moaning for more." I barely hear him, whimpering with sheer need and *bozhe moy*, there's *more* of him? There's no end to his shaft, even when it feels like I can't take any more.

"Yes, you can," he whispers diabolically, "you can take more. You can take all of me, even if you're crying and shaking because you want the pain along with how good I can make you feel. You love it, delicious, dirty girl. Because you're perfect."

He grips my ass, digging his fingers in and slams in and out of me, chuckling low when I come once, and then again when he pulls from me quickly, coming into the water. My head's drooping, forehead resting on his shoulder and his cock stays hard. Rock hard, like he didn't just come. He thrusts back inside my stretched, stinging channel, the water splashing around us.

"Let's see how much this pussy can take."

CHAPTER TWENTY

In which Cameron redeems himself. Mostly.

Cameron...

"Tell him we'll be there at noon. That isn't important. He'll make us another one."

Morana's dozing on one of the big wicker chairs in the pool house while I make some calls. I'd bundled her up in one of the big terrycloth robes we keep in here and I'm in another, pacing along the tile length of the pool.

Between beating the truth out of Ivanov and obsessing over my wife who hates me, I haven't slept more than a couple of hours in the last forty-eight. Still, I feel surprisingly energized. I haven't won Morana over yet. But the realization that I want to is sending a new strength through me. There's room left for something other than hate and revenge in my heart after all.

Now, if I can convince her to make room in her heart for me...

"Where are you taking me?"

She's looking out the window of my new, bulletproof Maserati SUV. I've had enough of my Range Rovers dying on me without any reason why. I've had more automotive bullshite in the last month than I've dealt with in my entire life.

My wife is wearing a pretty dress I had Miss Kevin put out for her, a pale violet that matches the bright tones in her eyes. Her blonde hair is smooth over her shoulders and I made her put her wedding ring - which I found shoved in a drawer in her bedside table - back on her hand.

"You've not been out of the house for a while. I'm taking you to lunch. We just have a bit of business first." She's eyeing me the way you look at deviled eggs left out in the sun. Squinty and suspicious.

We're turning into Parliament Square and she stares out the window at the stern, grey edifice of the Edinburgh City Chambers. It is impressive looking. However, given that my family owns most of the city council members makes it all a little less majestic to me.

Helping her out of the car, I enjoy the little frown she's wearing. "What are we doing here?"

"Paperwork."

"Why, if it isn't Mr. and Mrs. Cameron MacTavish!" The Lord Provost of Edinburgh rises to greet us as we're guided into his chambers.

"Hello, Alan. I need your help with a bit of bureaucracy," I say smoothly.

"Oh? How can I help?" He smiles at Morana a bit lecherously and I want to punch his expensive dental work down his throat.

"My sweet bride was tooling around online and wanted to look up our marriage license. You can imagine her disappointment when she couldn't find it."

"Cameron..." she hisses, her pretty face flushing red.

"Oh, I'm sorry, dear. It can take up to eight weeks for many official documents to be registered properly. I can send a clerk down to bring you a copy if you wish."

"Oh, that's not-"

"Yes," I cut in, "we would appreciate it."

It might take two months for his clerks to get their paperwork sorted but less than ten minutes for a puffing city employee to hurry into Baird's office with our marriage license.

"Yes, you see? Dated three weeks ago, Mrs. MacTavish," he smiles weakly at Morana, who's looking over the paperwork dubiously.

"Thank you, Graham," Baird says, waving him off. "Well then, is there anything else I can do for you, my friends?"

"Yes," I slide my arm around her waist. "I would like you to marry us."

He frowns, "But, as you see, you two are already-"

"I'd like you to marry us again," I interrupt.

"You'd like a renewal of your vows," he clarifies.

"Yes, and another certificate."

"Cameron, this is ridiculous," Morana whispers.

"Not in the slightest, darling," I kiss her hand, smiling down at her mortified face.

Baird shrugs. "Well, of course." Calling in his assistant as a witness, he gives a stirring speech about the sanctity of marriage - entertaining from a man that I have on video cavorting around a hotel room in his boxers with two women young enough to be his daughters - and turns us to look at each other.

"Please repeat after me: 'I, Cameron MacTavish, do solemnly and sincerely declare that I know of no legal impediment to my marrying...'" he checks his notes, "Morana Ivanova MacTavish.'"

I say the words, lingering over her name.

He repeats the same to Morana, and even though that little frown is still planted between her eyebrows, she says the words.

"Your second declaration today is where you shall accept each other in marriage. Please now join both your hands together."

When I take my wife's hands they're chilly, and shaking just a bit. Squeezing them gently, I bend my head to meet her perplexed gaze.

"Cameron, please make this declaration to Morana, 'I solemnly and sincerely declare that I, Cameron Torquil MacTavish, accept you, Morana Ivanova MacTavish, as my lawful wedded wife to the exclusion of all others.'"

I speak, and he has her repeat the phrases, which she does, haltingly, but without hesitation. There was one moment when I wondered if she would refuse.

Baird is heading into the home stretch and looks a little relieved. "You have now both entered a solemn and binding contract and by the virtue of these declarations made in my presence and the presence of the witness, I have pleasure in pronouncing you husband and wife.

"You may now kiss."

I cradle her delicate face in my hands and kiss my wife with a certain level of savagery that she seems to appreciate, based on the little noises that I'm sure she's not aware that she's making.

"Congratulations to you both," the Lord Provost says warmly.

"What just happened?" Morana's holding two wedding certificates on her lap.

"We got married again," I remind her. "You were there for both of them, as I recall. So, Mrs. MacTavish, I'm taking you to lunch and then back to the house for another wedding night."

By the time we make it to our table at The Witchery, Morana looks ready to stab me with her butter knife. I introduce her as my wife to the maître d', the sommelier, three business associates who happen to be dining there, and the busboy.

"I get the message, thank you," she whispers, looking around uncomfortably. "We're married. It's clear."

I smile innocently as I open the menu. "Try the trout, it's amazin' here."

After lunch, Morana relaxes enough with a glass of wine to eye me speculatively over the rim as she takes a sip. "What is the next step in your master plan?"

She already looked around to make certain we were alone, though I'd specified that I wanted a table in an alcove facing the entrance and away from everyone else.

"Keep taking everything away from two particular Bratvas, and when there's nothing left, kill them all," I say, finishing my glass of Maclellan Cask Strength Red Label.

"How dangerous is this for you and your family?"

"We have allies," I say, "those two have been mucking around in somebody else's playground. Other Bratvas who are not happy to hear it. Now that I have the proof, they're ready to align with us."

"I should feel something, shouldn't I?"

"What do you mean?"

"You just told me that you're going to wipe out the Ivanov line," she says slowly. "I should feel... sad? Angry? Something? But I don't."

"I saw your expression when you realized your Da' was in the Red Trade longer than you knew. You looked like you were going to be sick. Human traffickers are a pestilence that must be wiped out. I'm not a good man. But I'd never sell a human soul. And neither would you."

The weak sunlight is shining through the window, lighting her skin, and making her glow. "This morning you said that if I'd known about those girls, I would have let you kidnap me and draw in my cousin willingly. You are right. I would have. You never trusted me enough to give me the chance. You want me to trust you, husband. So, prove it by trusting me. Whatever I know, however I can help, I'll do it gladly. But ask me."

I lightly tap my glass to hers. "Aye. That's fair." I feel shame for the first time in… I don't know. Looking at her serious little face, I know I fucked up big, and an additional wedding in a bureaucrat's office is not going to be enough to make up for it.

CHAPTER TWENTY-ONE

In which the sex is so good.

Morana...

I'm lying face down on Cameron's bed, and I can't move. Not a toe. Not a finger.

He made good on his promise (threat?) to bring me home for another wedding night. There are floor-to-ceiling windows in the master bedroom, and pulling over one of his big armchairs, he placed it in front of them and lifted me to straddle him, still in my dress, ripping my undies off. He played with my center with his fingers while his other hand pulled down the top of my dress to lick and bite my nipples. When he decided I was wet enough to take him, he slid me down his dick, pushing on the small of my back to rub his piercing hard against my swollen clitoris.

"Shhh... let me do the work," he whispered diabolically, not thrusting, just circling my hips, buried inside me so that his cock pushed against that wild bundle of nerves inside as the hard metal of his piercing stroked over my clitoris. Over, and over until I was nearly boneless with need and nearly crying for relief.

"So close..." I moaned and when I squeezed down on him, he slapped my ass hard.

"Don't you try to make me cum," he warned, gripping me tighter. Each time I started to contract against his cock buried inside me, he spanked me again. He spanked me until my skin was bright red and searing hot and finally, that's what sent me over the edge, weeping and biting his shoulder to bury my screams.

"My poor bride..." he's leaning over me, running his warm hand against my sore ass. "I spanked you raw, didn't I? I have something for that."

He's still shamelessly naked and I'm staring at his dick, which is possibly still half-hard. I still can't believe he got that inside me. I want to see if he can do it again. I don't care how sore I am.

I groan a little as I feel something cool sweep over my chafed skin. "That feels better."

"Speaking of feelings," he leers, "do you feel good and married now?"

"Yes, you ass. I believe you. We're married. *Legally.*"

"Good!" Suddenly, he's all business. "Because if we don't show up to the family estate on Sunday for dinner, my mother is going to be displeased. Believe me when I say you do not want to see Elspeth MacTavish displeased."

Cameron...

She turns away from me, curling on her side.

Ah. "You feel uncomfortable because of the nightclub maneuver, thinking everyone knew you were the bait?"

She pulls the sheet up over her shoulders.

"Not uncomfortable. Humiliated. Shamed."

"*Mo fhlùr...* If it makes any difference, Mala thought we should have told you from the beginning. She comes from a horrible feckin' family, too. You'll have a lot in common," I say dryly. "Very few people knew. My brothers. The bodyguards. No one is laughing at you and thinking of you as less."

"I've just barely accepted…" she rolled over again, waving her hand at me, "…this. I feel like I'm orbiting a new sun, everything is different. The last three weeks have felt like suspended animation, waiting to see what was going to happen." My bride sits up, wincing at the pressure on her sore ass and pulling the sheet up to cover her breasts, an action I note with some regret. "Now you want me to play 'Meet the Family' and pretend everything is normal when nothing is."

"That's understandable," I agree. She's right. "We can start slow. Would you like to have lunch with Mala first, get to know her a little? You can swap stories about fathers who are shite and arranged marriages to lecherous old bastards."

"Are you calling yourself a lecherous old bastard?" She sasses me.

"I'm talking about the other one, ya' Bessie! I'm only twelve years older than you."

"Really? You're thirty-two?" She frowns thoughtfully. "That's so old. And what's a Bessie?"

"A rude, bad-tempered woman, which ye' are," I say sternly. "And here I am bein' all kind and understanding and shite."

She gives a little giggle and it's so fecking charming that I want to hear it again. Immediately. I like her unguarded smile, how she sets down the persona that protected her for so long. Like maybe she feels safe enough with me to finally do it.

Then my smile fades.

"I have to leave again."

"Oh?" At least she looks disappointed.

"Aye, we're at a sensitive juncture with a key shipping route for the Stepanov Bratva. If we close this off, it drives them further out of Moscow."

"Where are you driving them to?" Morana asks.

"Good question. In World War Two, the Scottish Highlander battalions were called *Die Damen aus der Hölle* by the Nazis."

She chuckles, "I know a little German… the Ladies from Hell?"

"Aye. The Highlanders would wear their kilts and play their war pipes and they were known to be so ferocious in battle that the Nazi troops would flee before them when they heard the bagpipes."

Smiling, she nods. "I remember my history lessons, back when the Russians and the Scottish were on the same side in World War Two, our people had great admiration for the Scot's tactics. So how does this relate here?"

"Well, a regiment used this specific tactic we have in play, in a particularly difficult battle in occupied Italy. The Germans were tearing the country apart. The Scottish troops - they were called the Cameronians - drove the Nazis into a valley that ended in a blind canyon, with more sharpshooters lying in wait on the cliffs."

"That's genius," she says.

"Less than two hundred Scots killed over a thousand Germans that day."

My bride's eyes are wide, "And that's what you're doing with the Stepanov and Ivanov Bratvas?"

Grinning in a way that feels feral, I nod. "Exactly. But without the war pipes. And more explosives."

CHAPTER TWENTY-TWO

In which Morana has a clue.

Morana...

Even though the master bedroom feels empty when I wake up, for the first time in a long time, I have something to look forward to.

Cameron, that overbearing ass, already registered me back at the Royal Danish Academy, and even though it's mid-term, my professors are suspiciously open to helping me catch up. There's a comfortable little area off the master bedroom suite, and I was escorted there today by a beaming Miss Kevin to find a desk set up with a view of the back gardens and the oak tree with the swing. There's an alarmingly expensive MacBook already set up with every possible study accessory covering the desk.

I'd tried to go back to my old room to change, but our ever-helpful butler cleared her throat. "Ah, you will find that your things have been moved into the master bedroom. Should you need more space, there is also an alcove on the other side of the suite that could be converted into another dressing room."

The one I'm apparently now sharing with Cameron is larger than some third-world countries, so I'm not sure how much room she thinks I could possibly need. "Thank you, Miss Kevin, this is all... very over the top and signature 'Master MacTavish,' but truly, *spasibo*. Thank you for all the time you've spent setting this up. It's wonderful."

Then she does something that is so nice. Very gently, she pats my arm. The touch almost makes me cry and I realize that other than the filthy sexual congress I've been getting up to with my husband, no one has touched me. Not like a friend. Like someone who cares.

Miss Kevin leans forward, speaking precisely, but gently. "I am so very happy you are here."

She leaves the room before I can cry and make a complete fool of myself, and then I find Bad Cat so I can lavish the rest of my unseemly emotion upon him.

"How was your day?"

I get an illicit thrill when Cameron Facetimed me. It was late and I was eyeing his huge, comfortable bed when the call came in.

"Good," I say happily, "thank you for registering me even though I was perfectly capable of registering myself, but there's-"

"I wanted to make it easy so you could get started right away," he interrupts, "I know you've missed your classes."

"Okay, thank you again but-"

"Is your new study comfortable? We can set you up in the library if you'd prefer-"

"Okay Cameron I need you to listen for a moment!" I thunder.

His brow goes up. "Fine lass, ya' don't need to get all Bessie about it."

"I can tell I'm really going to hate that phrase soon. Please hear me out. I told you that my father never talked business when I was around, right? But I remembered something that could possibly be of help?" I hate that the sentence comes out like a question as if I really am a useless Bratva princess.

Cameron's tired, I can tell but his attention is focused on me.

"I was going over study notes today and reading about Ivan Aivazovsky, he's one of the most famous maritime painters from

Russia."

"Go on," he's rubbing his eyes.

"Then, I remembered a conversation between my father and a couple of his brigadiers. They were making a joke about how useful Aivazovsky's work was, because he'd painted one picture from a port that was no longer in use, and it was perfect for late-night shipments."

Leaning forward, he nods, smiling warmly. "My clever wife. You know where the artist painted that picture, don't you?"

"Yes!" I bounce a little, "It's an oceanfront location about fifteen miles from St. Petersburg, just outside the town of Sosnovy Bor. When Aivazovsky wrote about that painting, he praised the location for its 'peaceful desolation.' It would be ideal because there's even a railway system close by."

"If you were here right now I would make you come until you lost consciousness," he blurts. "It's genius. It's something that even O'Rourke didn't know. My brilliant, clever wife."

"It's just a lead, it may not go anywhere," I shrug, "but I'm happy I thought of something that might help."

He leans back against the pillows on his bed. His hand not holding the phone is moving lower and I press my lips together. "Where are ya' at, lass?"

Turning the camera around, I show him the master bedroom and the absurdly large bed before panning back to me. "I'm bouncing on your very comfortable mattress. This bed is the size of an ocean liner, by the way."

"Sweet Jesus I wish I was bouncin' on that bed with you," he groans before his smile turns devilish. "Show me what you're wearing, my pretty, filthy wife."

CHAPTER TWENTY-THREE

In which there is dinner with an unsettling billionaire.

Cameron...

"Get packed, I'm takin' you on a trip."

My pretty bride's face lights up like a Christmas tree. I've taken to Facetiming her each night after another day of going through the dregs of Moscow, killing Stepanov men.

Today's raid on one of their holding cells was particularly bad.

"Really?" Morana, "When are you coming home?"

Something glows in me when she says "home." As in mine, and hers.

"I'm flying into Dublin in the morning, and you're meetin' me there, lass. Fancy having dinner with Nolan O'Rourke at his legendary whiskey distillery?"

"Can we have dinner, but without O'Rourke?" she asks flatly. "He's unsettling."

"Unsettling!" I snap my fingers, "I've been searchin' for the right word. We still need to have dinner with him though, unsettling or no."

"All right," she agrees unenthusiastically before brightening hopefully. "Could we maybe walk around a bit after? I've never been to Dublin."

"Aye, we can do that." It feels good to grant her wishes, and she asks for so little. For a girl raised in the pampered oasis of a Russian crime family, Morana is surprisingly unspoiled.

She's looking at me closely, a little frown between her eyebrows. "You look like today was a bad day. Well, every day has been horrible for you since you landed in Moscow, but..." she pauses, "today was worse?"

"It was." I hesitate. "The holding cell, it was in the Golyanovo District."

She winces. "I hope you got a tetanus shot."

"Not a bad idea." The doctor's been and gone already, patching up a bullet wound in my thigh and it's aching like a motherfucker. "There were forty cages, no bigger than a dog's crate." She's listening in silence, her gaze never leaving mine. "They were all full, but only twenty-five of 'em were alive."

Tears instantly spring to her eyes.

"Some of the kids, they couldn't have been more than thirteen or fourteen," I stumble on, not sure why I can't shut up. "One of the girls who made it, she was holding hands through the bars with her sister in the next cage. We had to..." I run my hand through my hair. "We had to sedate her to make her let go. Her sister didn't..."

"*O, Bozhe*, dear God," she sobs, "I am so sorry. For those poor girls. For you to see it. For everything. I wish I could take this memory away and carry it for you."

"Each time we rescue these kids, I see Sorcha's face, my little sister's face. If Cormac hadn't gotten to her in time, she could have been one of those girls," I ramble on. "She was kidnapped by a Triad because the MacTavish Clan wouldn't let them ship human cargo through our ports.

"They took her, my aunt, and my little cousins. After we got 'em back, we went after the Triad. We killed every one of them. Every. One. But the Stepanov Bratva is the second half of their operation. Until Vadik Stepanov and your Da' are bone and ash, I'll still see her face."

129

I can sense her sorrow. Just from seeing her expression, I know she feels what I do.

"For the rest of their lives, these girls will remember you," she says firmly, "they'll remember the moment the door opened and light came in. The light was you. They'll see your face in their dreams and the moment they realized they were safe. God willing, they won't think of when they were taken, but of when you saved them. They'll remember the light."

I lightly tap the phone against my forehead and get myself under control.

"I wish I was there with you," she whispers.

"I do, too." I didn't mean to say it out loud.

Morana...

"Well, this is exciting," Mala teases, "a real date!"

"Not when we have to have dinner with Nolan O'Rourke," I snort, throwing another shirt in my overnight bag. "There's something so wrong about that man."

"Yeah," she agrees casually, "he's a sociopath and he'd blow up the world for laughs if he ever got his hands on a big enough nuke."

"That's... not a pep talk if that's what you were going for, just so you know."

"Sorry." Mala did seem apologetic. "It's easy to joke when I'm not the one having to hang out with him all night. Do you want to have lunch when you get back?"

"That would be nice." Instead of the chilly anxiety I usually feel when I think about dealing with Cameron's family, this is warming, a cautious optimism that makes me think there might actually be a place for me here.

"Good!" She's all business. "Now, finish packing and throw in some extra lingerie."

"We're not at that point in our sister-in-law relationship yet," I primly reply, "I must ask you to refrain from such language."

She laughs raucously, as I expect. "Yeah, tell it to someone who's not married to one of these horny bastards. Have fun in Ireland!"

I hang up, a little flustered. Well, Cameron did buy drawers and drawers of this stuff… marching into the closet, I grab a fistful of silk and lace without looking and put it into the bag, zipping it up before I change my mind.

"Ah, the lovely Morana *Ivanova* MacTavish," purrs Nolan O'Rourke as he stands to greet us.

Trying not to glare, I say, "I just go by MacTavish now, thank you."

He puts a courtly hand to the chest of his $10,000 bespoke suit made of unicorn skins or something close. "Oh, but it is a shame to lose touch with one's heritage."

"Not my Russian heritage," I force myself to speak calmly, he knows he's getting to me, "just the family line. I'm sure you understand, based on recent events."

He smiles fondly, opening his mouth and showing off all his perfect teeth, and Cameron cuts in. "O'Rourke, good to see your distillery at last. You acquired it after that O'Connell massacre, correct? And then the fire. Tragic, that." My husband doesn't bother to lower his voice.

None of this seems to upset our host. I knew the MacTavish Clan were billionaires. But I can't imagine the level of money it would take to be as supremely carefree and untouchable as Nolan O'Rourke.

He merely chuckles indulgently and waves at the table. "Join me."

The table is built into an alcove in the old distillery, a perfect shadowy balcony that oversees the dining room below it and all the gleaming copper pot stills and oak fermenting barrels. Cameron told me on the way over that there was some cataclysmic fire shortly after O'Rourke acquired it, but everything looks like it has been here for the 150 years the distillery has been in operation.

"I asked the chef to throw something together for tonight," O'Rourke says casually. "I stole him from a little place in Paris and he brought their Michelin stars with him. The restaurant in question closed last month. Sadly, it doesn't seem they survived his departure."

"When you say… you stole him," I ask cautiously, "traditionally, I would assume you lured him away with an obscene amount of money and cart blanche over the menu. But, you being you…"

He laughs heartily, barely a wrinkle to be seen on his perfect skin. Did he buy it from a twenty-year-old? Didn't Cameron say he was in his late forties? "Your scenario is correct, dear. Although had he played coy, I might have considered stronger measures."

Fortunately, the waiter interrupts this troubling discussion with a tartare of scallops, pomelo, shisho, elderflower, and horseradish.

Taking a bite, I give out an involuntary moan. Leaning close, Cameron whispers, "The next time I hear that comin' out of your mouth, we'd better be in bed, lass."

The wonderful meal almost turns to ash in my mouth when the men begin a discussion on what they're calling the "final assault" on the Stepanov Bratva, and by association, my father's. This is a real shame because the next course is BBQ Donegal lobster with carrot and citrus sauce.

By the time we're finished with the wild strawberries, poached meringue, lovage, and Voatsiperifery pepper, I'm prepared to overlook all of O'Rourke's faults if I can eat here every day for the rest of my life.

"I do hope you're not uncomfortable, darling." O'Rourke is cradling a glass of brandy and looking at me with a ridiculously insincere expression of concern. "We are speaking of your father's end, of course."

I think of Cameron's pain last night. The story of the two sisters. "I would end him myself if given the chance."

He doesn't ask me again.

CHAPTER TWENTY-FOUR

In which Cameron is just absurdly romantic.

Morana...

"Well, that was interesting," I venture.

"That would be one way to put it," Cameron agrees dryly.

We're walking hand in hand in Iveagh Gardens, a secret paradise in the middle of the city. "This reminds me a lot of what Central Park was meant to be in New York City," I say, "but magical in a way that can only come from being three hundred years old with waterfalls and a proper yew maze."

"Look at you, ya' beautiful botanist," he grins, leaning down for a kiss. He made up for two hours of Nolan O'Rourke's company by taking me to Love Lane to see the artwork inspired by shameless romantics and then this beautiful place.

"Do you feel like..." I'm searching for the right way to ask something so serious, even though I know it's going to ruin this beautiful bubble he's created for me. "Are you on the right course? Do you know where this is all going to end?"

Cameron gives me the courtesy of thinking about it. "Aye. I've gone over this battle plan with my brothers and our lieutenants for countless hours. I can recite every move, every step, it's ingrained in my memory so deep I'll never pry it out again. We have gone over every action and counter-move they could make. I know how this will end. And it will be soon."

He slows to a stop, holding my hands. "I dinna' want this to overshadow the rest of our night."

"I know. I'm grateful though, and oddly, I'm happy."

Frowning, he cocks his head. "How so, wife?"

"Because you trusted me with the truth, and because I should have seen this so much sooner. I should have known," I say sadly. "I could have tried to help these girls, maybe I could have saved so many of them if I'd not been so stubbornly blind."

"No, you dinna' blame yourself. Ivanov kept you away at school for all those years for a reason. He would never risk you discovering what he was doing and making a run for it. He wanted to keep you complacent, right up to the point he sold you off to that vile old feck Stepanov. But now ya' know. And you have already been invaluable."

"I want to do more," I say. "Will you train me to be stronger? I can go on missions with you, or work with these girls in rebuilding their lives."

"Lass, ya' need not-"

"No, husband. I do. I have to redeem myself for all those years I knew nothing. When I did nothing."

Cameron smiles down at me, and there's light in his eyes that illuminates him and makes me see what those terrified girls must experience when he rescues them. A second chance at life.

"I have one more place to show you tonight," he says, kissing me tenderly.

"Oh?" It's nearly midnight and I've been thinking a lot about that enormous suite he booked for us at the Clontarf Castle Hotel.

"We canna leave Dublin without paying homage to the patron saint of lovers," Cameron grins, pulling me into the Carmelite Church. It's closed, but a priest is waiting for us by the massive front doors.

"Welcome, my children. I'm Father O'Cleary. I understand you would like to take a moment at the shrine of Saint Valentine?"

I grin up at my suddenly romantic husband. "Thank you, Father, we would."

We stand together in front of the shrine with the beautiful painting of St. Valentine in robes of red and white gazing down on us, and the smell of roses and beeswax candles perfume the air. There's such a peace here, a comforting presence. Finally, Father O'Cleary gently clears his throat. "There is one last place your husband wished you to see."

We walk in the tiny chapel to the front of the altar, a glowing pathway of candles guiding our way.

"I- what's happening?" I look around awkwardly, unsure what I'm expected to do.

"I would like to marry you, Mrs. MacTavish," Cameron says gravely.

Barely stopping myself from rolling my eyes, which seems very disrespectful in front of this kindly priest, I say, "We are. Married, I mean. You convinced me of that, you know."

"Aye," he kisses my hand, "but I will always want to marry you again."

This is… so absurdly, beautifully romantic that I'm speechless. They both wait for me to regain my senses, and I nod, trying not to break into a round of unseemly tears. We say our vows again, he slips my ring back on my finger and I carefully place his wedding band back on his.

Looking at his beautiful face in the candlelight, I know that when I spoke the vows of love tonight, I truly meant them.

CHAPTER TWENTY-FIVE

In which there is so much sex.

Morana...

They've barely closed our car door when Cameron is mauling me like a starved bear, and I attack him in return. I'm grateful there's a privacy screen rising between us and a stone-faced Hamish, who is desperately trying to keep his eyes away from the rearview mirror.

"I was plannin' a romantic seduction moment back at the hotel," Cameron groans in my ear.

"We can do that too," I agree, sliding my fingers into his silky hair and gripping it. "But I have a lot of good feelings toward you right now."

Sliding between his legs and kneeling on the floor, my hands go to his belt buckle before he stops me. "Ya' don't have to do this, wife."

"I... probably won't be any good at it," I admit, "but I want to."

"You're killin' me," he groans, ripping his pants open and raising his hips to help me pull down his boxer briefs.

"Was it always this big?" I blurt, cringing when he tries to smother his chuckle. Somehow, seeing him up close is different than on Facetime, where he's lured me into doing all sorts of naughtiness on our nightly calls. My husband is huge; thick and hot, and it's throbbing softly in my hand.

"Tighten your hand," he urges, "squeeze it."

I do, and my tongue comes out to lick up the pearl that beads from the tip. He tastes sharp, feels silky on my tongue. Cameron always smells good, but here where I couldn't be closer to him, he smells... warm. He smells like how warm would feel, and for a girl with chilly Russian blood, it's the most luxurious of things.

His groan is so rewarding that I do it again, and stretch my lips around him, my tongue sliding along the bottom of him and feeling the vein pulsing there. This is so abruptly, intensely erotic that my other hand makes its way between my legs, pushing against my undies, feeling them getting wet.

With another deep breath through my nose, I push harder, feeling him against the back of my throat and choke a bit, pulling back. When I suck him back in, I'm prepared and concentrate on the feel of him, the weight, and how hot he is. Squeezing experimentally, I enjoy his groan and try it again while I suck on him harder. I'm aware of how wet and messy it sounds, the spit and pre-cum leaking from the corners of my mouth but when Cameron swipes a finger along my jaw and collects it, I swear he gets harder.

"You're so feckin' beautiful," he growls. His hands are under my arms and I'm abruptly lifted to straddle him. "Such a bad girl," he whispers diabolically, "your fingers in that pretty little pussy. But it belongs to me, and you'll come on my cock or you won't come at all."

He rips my undies off as I yelp, and the head of his shaft is just inside me and he grins, squeezing my ass. "Slide down, lass. As slow or fast as ye' like. Ride me. Use my cock until you come."

He's so wet from me, and I'm shockingly slick and we both moan as I push down on him hard, clear to the base of him, feeling his piercing rubbing my clitoris. "Just- give me a moment," I wheeze.

"Take your time," he grunts, "Hamish will circle the feckin' hotel until we're done."

This makes me giggle, which rubs the piercing harder against me and oh, I'm embarrassed to be coming so fast, him throbbing inside me like a thick spike, our mouths together and breath mingling. My back arches as I come with a hoarse cry, fingers digging into his pristine white shirt and hearing his guttural chuckle.

"Just like that, my beautiful, filthy wife."

He gives me a second or two to catch my breath, then thrusts viciously up, shoving his shaft up into me, his hands gripping my ass tighter to push me down. It hurts, he's at the top of my channel, with nowhere else to go but he keeps pounding into me.

"I'll make it fit," he says, biting my neck, "I'll shape your cunt to fit only me, I'll fuck you until not having me inside is painful, too empty." Cameron pulls out, then slams back in again. "You are fucking built for me, sweet wife." His hands slide to my waist, yanking me even farther onto his dick. "So perfect, love. So snug."

When he finally erupts inside me, I convulse, coming again and clamping down hard on him. He's right, I want to keep him inside me forever.

The sound of our harsh breaths finally brings me back to some kind of awareness of our surroundings. "Where are we?" I mumble, burrowing into his warm chest.

"On the fifth or sixth loop of the hotel, I'm thinking," he chuckles. He gently lifts me off him and helps me tidy up, pocketing my torn undies with a little wink. I want to glare at him but I'm feeling dangerously soft after those two orgasms.

Much later, after Cameron has reinforced my earlier two orgasms with three more, he's holding me up in the shower, washing my back.

"We're three-times married," I sigh, "I guess there's no running away now."

"Plus, you know you'd miss that thing I do with my tongue," he agrees.

He cups my face, kissing me, and when I put my hands over his, I feel the swelling.

"Wait, what happened here?" Gently holding his wrists, I see more tally marks like the ones I'd been so alarmed by when he first kidnapped me. There are twenty new tattooed marks, fresh against the reddened skin on his right wrist, and two on his left. "What is this?"

I'm so used to seeing grinning, smart-assed Cameron that his somber expression is jolting. "These are the men I've killed in service to the MacTavish Clan," he says, holding up his right hand. Showing me his left wrist, he lets me touch the marks gently. "And these are for the clansmen I have lost."

There must be a hundred tally marks on his right. A hundred. He must be an executioner for the MacTavish Mafia, my sunny-natured husband. I'm grateful to see less than twenty on his left. I try to count them silently, and he pulls his hand away.

"Losing Ferr and ten soldiers… it was the worst moment of my life," he says. "Afterward, I was stupid, I took too many risks, trying to make Stepanov pay. Cormac and Dougal had to hold me down one night and beat the shite out of me before I'd listen to reason."

"Was I part of this new plan?"

"You were," he said, water beading against his skin and sticking his unreasonably thick eyelashes together.

"Would you really have stuck that needle in my eye?" I ask.

Rolling his eyes, he kisses me, hard. "What do you think, wife?"

"You were very convincing at the time," I mumble.

Kissing down my neck, he chuckles. "Good to know."

"So, how was it?"

Since all I've been thinking about is the sex marathon Cameron and I had in Dublin, I choke a bit at Mala's question.

"Um, his jet had a problem and we were stranded on the runway for three hours and there was a freak lightning storm as we were trying to land in Edinburgh, but other than that, it was pretty good," I mumble.

"Uh, huh," she says, her amusement clear. "Doesn't Cameron's jet have a bedroom in the back?"

"What does that have to do with anything?" I take another bite of my salmon, avoiding her entertained gaze.

"Nothing. So how was dinner with Nolan O'Rourke?"

"Much less fun than this one," I sigh, "he enjoyed mocking me about my family. As if I'm not ashamed enough."

"Hey," she points her fork at me. "If anyone understands being ashamed of their family, it's me. But you have a new family now, one to be proud of. I know you had a rough start, and I'm sorry I couldn't make it easier on you. There *is* something here to build on, something you can be proud of."

The oceanside restaurant we're eating at is weathered and beautiful, just like the shore. The rare Edinburgh sun is out and warm on my shoulders. Both Natalia and Mala's personal security are seated at the table just behind us, clearly bored with their work.

My life has been so regimented until now, and I used to think about casual lunches out with friends as something unattainable, that only normal people got to do. No one at University who knew about my background wanted anything to do with me, and the other Bratva princesses were deadly. I approached each social event with them like walking a tightrope over a pit of vipers.

"Oh!" Mala continues, "Cameron asked me if I could train with you."

"Really?" I brighten up. "He's been sparring with me but he's been out of town so much that my progress is pitiful. You were some kind of a super spy at the Ares Academy, weren't you? I'm warning you, I know maybe three moves. You could probably kill me without getting out of your chair."

"Oh, honey," laughs Mala, "we're going to have so much fun. Learning to fight like a woman is much easier than learning how to fight like a man. They don't get it. You'll see what I mean."

I tilt my face up to the sun and smile. A fresh start. A sister-in-law. Finally, a sense of purpose.

CHAPTER TWENTY-SIX

In which we – awkwardly – Meet the Family.

Morana...

"You're tensing up," Cameron glances over at me. "Stop tensing."

"I can't stop tensing!" I shift in my seat, too anxious to appreciate the perfection of the vintage Jaguar my husband is driving. For once, the car started up perfectly, purring like a kitten. I guess even my grim Russian karmic misfortune is no match for a 1961 E-Type Roadster in forest green.

Cameron attempted to distract me from my rising anxiety by telling me all the features of his most treasured car. All I knew was that this beautiful thing took every turn in the winding road to his parent's estate like it was made for this moment. The purr of the engine, the wind tearing through my hair was almost enough to keep me from panicking about meeting his family.

"Did you drive the Jaguar today to distract me?" I demanded.

"Is it working?"

"I'm mainly worried that my bad luck doesn't kill it somehow, so I guess that counts."

He looks over again, so handsome in his Ray Bans. "What are you talking about?"

"I told you! I'm bad luck. My name means 'death,' remember?"

"You know that all that nasty shite is from your father, right? There's nothing wrong with you, lass." Cameron expertly makes another turn, nearly losing the two SUVs following us.

"What about your Bugatti? I killed your Bugatti," I persist.

"A tree fell on my Bugatti," he sighs.

"The flat tire when you kidnapped me? How do all your brand-new cars keep dying for no reason?"

"You're not bad luck, Morana! If anything, you're good luck. Thanks to you, we found that fucker Stepanov's last stand, his hidden compound. We are almost done with a battle that's raged on for over five years. Because of you, honey." He puts his big, warm hand on my thigh and I scream.

"Look out!"

Cursing, he swerves just in time to avoid five sheep casually crossing the road. The Jaguar nearly spins out, but the tires catch in time.

"See?"

"God-*damnit* it's not your fault!" Cameron roars.

The cloudy skies open up, dumping rain down on us and he hits the button to bring the ragtop up on the convertible.

Nothing.

Growling, he pushes it again and again, and I sigh, hoping the vintage camel tan leather interior isn't ruined by the time we get to the estate.

When we show up for dinner, soaking wet, there is an acutely uncomfortable moment as they all stand in the grand hall, beautifully dressed.

Staring at me.

"Sorcha darling," Lady Elspeth says, "do take Morana up to your room for some dry things?"

"Thanks for the clothes."

"You're welcome." Sorcha, Cameron's little sister is lounging on her bed, grinning at me.

I like this girl, she's sassy and funny. As she shares her clothes with me and I attempt to look more presentable, she keeps up a stream of cheerful chatter about the family and their most embarrassing moments. Sorcha's only eighteen, but she's wildly beautiful, with thick waves of auburn hair and that perfect, pale skin that you can only find here in Scotland.

And she's refused to leave the estate since she was kidnapped when she was twelve.

"So, is it as awkward as you were expecting?" she asks, looking at me upside down as she hangs her head over the mattress.

Surprised into a laugh, I nod, drying my hair. "Pretty much what I was expecting. It's still nice to meet you, though."

"Oh, we're all fun, aside from the towering presence of Ma," she says, "even Da is so much more relaxed since giving the Chieftain title over to Cormac. Besides, you are not the most awkward wifey introduction we've had."

"What do you mean?"

A knock on the door interrupts us and Mala slips in. "She means me. I showed up at midnight and Cormac announced that he was going to marry me. Lady Elspeth had a wedding for one hundred people ready on the grounds here at the estate by five o'clock the next afternoon. I think I win this round."

"That's impressive," I admit, "and much more elegant than essentially being held down by your brother while your parish priest reluctantly pronounces us husband and wife."

"I did wonder how that happened!" Sorcha says happily. "Tell me more!"

"Later," Mala warns, "Lady Elspeth is becoming displeased. Also,

Cameron is chasing my twins around and getting them all riled up. He's still a child himself, I swear."

That galvanized Sorcha to leap from the bed and I quickly try to wipe off the mascara trailing down my face.

"I will tell you," I say as we hurry down the hall, "that your brother redeemed himself spectacularly by renewing our vows in a much more pleasant manner. Twice."

"I did not know the man had it in him," she marvels. "Cameron, a romantic?"

Dinner goes much better than I expected. Cormac Sr. has me sit next to him. He is as hugely imposing as his sons, but his age has mellowed him in the best way. He kindly engages me in conversation as I relax by small degrees to the point that I can finally put food in my mouth without choking.

"I feel as if I should apologize to you all," I whisper.

"And why would that be?" He leans closer.

"My father… the St- those people. They caused your family so much suffering." I'm twisting my napkin in my lap, the shame of it all suddenly hitting me. These people have been kind to me, they welcomed me in today so warmly.

"There are some syndicates that count the sins of the fathers onto the children," he says after a thoughtful pause. "We are not among them. Each generation is responsible for themselves. You have discovered the worst, and you did not hide away from it. You have redeemed yourself."

"How?" I ask, puzzled.

"This work is ugly," he sighs quietly. "It stains you in a way that never fades. After Cameron lost his second in command, I feared for him. Since he married you, I see my son again. I know you two talk, I know you comfort him. He needed you."

Shaking my head, I manage a tremulous little smile. "I'm not sure I deserve that, but thank you."

Patting my arm, Cormac Sr. smiles warmly. "My dear, you deserve so much more. Have faith in our belief in you until you have it for yourself."

"I really like your father," I venture, getting ready for bed.

Cameron looks up from unbuttoning his shirt. "He likes you, I can tell. He never talks to anyone that long. The whole family approves of you, even Ma."

"Even after our completely ignominious entrance, dripping onto your mother's priceless rug?"

"Even then," he chuckles. "I think Lachlan nearly pissed himself trying not to laugh at her expression."

"This isn't helping my mood, in case you were heading in that direction."

"My poor lass," he soothes, his big hands suddenly roaming all over me.

"Is this where you unleash your deviance?" I ask, "Because I am completely open to that."

He pulls the strap of my camisole down, sucking my nipple into his mouth. Pushing me down on the bed, he attacks my breasts again. "*So* much deviance," he growls.

CHAPTER TWENTY-SEVEN

In which there are startling revelations.

Cameron...

Two months later...

Leaning back against the pillows, I try to stifle my groan.

"You sound like an octogenarian," my sassy bride says with a grin.

"Shut it. I had to beat the shite out of three arseholes when my gun ran out of bullets."

"Sorry," she says, half concerned and half smiling. "I'm so used to you pulling off magnificent feats of strength that I'm getting complacent. Where are you now?"

"Kazan, they've been using the Volga River to transport women from Volgograd. But after we got them out, we lit that dock area up," I say with satisfaction. "It will take them a week to get that fire out. Every warehouse and your father's trucking company are destroyed."

"That makes me very happy to hear," she says vehemently. "I do look forward to a future where I wake up in the same bed with you for more than a few days at a time." Her smile fades. "And now I feel guilty complaining about that when you're doing such important and, may I add, very dangerous work."

"Wife, I feel the same." My smile in the mirror is huge and likely looks a bit unhinged. I've only been able to be home and with - and inside - my wife for a week or so at a time before having to take off again, and hearing her admit she misses me... is she beginning to see the same future for us that I do? "How are your self-defense lessons going with Mala?"

She immediately brightens. "Really well, thank you for asking her! It helps to work with someone my size."

"I should have just had Natalia do it, but..." My wife is not as good at guarding her expressions as she used to be. "Are ye' not getting along with her?"

"It's not that, exactly," she says, "she does her job just fine. I am well-protected."

"Then what?"

"She despises me." Bad Cat is sitting on her lap and she starts stroking him, as if for comfort. "If I were her, maybe I would, too. I don't want to be in a position where we're forced to interact more than we are."

My jaw tightens. "She and her husband came very highly recommended, but no one treats my wife with disrespect. I'll replace her right away."

"Look, please don't worry about it! You need to concentrate completely on what you're doing. I'm fine. I'm safe, and I have my sisters-in-law to spend time with. I have a test for Slavic Art History that I need to study for. We can talk about any changes after this..."

Morana pauses, trying to think of the right way to say, 'After you kill my father and Stepanov and everyone associated with them and burn it all to the ground and then salt the earth.'

"After this mission," she settles on. "This is too important to be distracted by little things, all right?"

"Aye," I scowl. "But I don't like it."

"Don't we have something better to do?" She distracts me with a sly smile. "How would you like to desecrate our Facetime session tonight?"

My hand slides under my sweatpants. "I have a few ideas."

Morana...

"If you pull forward a little harder, you can get me off balance," Mala instructs. "Let's try this one more time."

She's been trying to teach me this maneuver all morning, and it's infuriating that I can't get this tiny woman to fly over my shoulder when she demonstrated it on a 200-pound guard.

"Let me get some water first..." Suddenly, just the thought of water hits me with a violent surge of nausea and I barely make it to the bathroom across the hall.

"There are easier ways of getting out of practice," Mala teases me gently, holding back my hair.

"*Bozhe moy,* this is so embarrassing," I groan, "don't look at me!"

"Please, you haven't seen anything until you've witnessed a post-Challenge party at the Ares Academy," she chuckles, "I've held the hair of every woman on campus and half the men." Her smile fades a bit. "Have you been getting sick a lot?"

"For the last couple of days," I say, rinsing out my mouth, "I might have a bug or maybe it's the haggis I had to try at Sunday dinner."

"That was four days ago," she laughs, "stop casting aspersions on traditional Scottish fare. I don't want to be pushy, but is it possible that you're pregnant? These MacTavish men are alarmingly fertile."

"No, we've always used..." Cameron has been very responsible about wearing a condom except... oh, *der'mo,* shit! That time in the car after getting married in Dublin.

"Your face is pale," Mala says sympathetically. "Why don't we go to lunch and make a quick stop at the drugstore?"

"This is bad," I moan, "we've only been married for four months! I can't be pregnant!" The dark fears surge up. My mother.

"Hey, hey, relax," she soothes me. "No freaking out until we know, all right?"

We leave Natalia and Mala's bodyguard standing by the door of the drugstore, bored out of their minds as Mala and I leisurely discuss the merits of the mauve vs. the berry shade of lipstick. She finally meanders to the cashier with a basketful of items, including three pregnancy tests.

"We'll go to a nice place for lunch," she whispers, "you do not want to take this test in the grimy restroom of the Boots Pharmacy."

"Good point," I smile weakly, stuffing the tests in my bag.

Mala kindly tries to distract me with chatter over my uneaten plate of Scottish shrimp and cherry blossom jam. The server comes by to see my lack of progress and looks personally wounded. "Is there something else I can bring you, ma'am?"

Mala blessedly intervenes. "That dark chocolate tart with candied hazelnuts looks delicious. Why don't you bring one for both of us?"

"I'm just going to visit the ladies' room," I casually announce.

Natalia goes first, of course, checking the stalls as an older woman with a massive wedding ring stares at her, bemused. When she leaves, Natalia moves to block the door and I groan.

"Please wait outside." When she looks stubborn, I pat my abdomen. "I've got an upset stomach and it won't be pretty."

She rolls her eyes discreetly and leaves me alone.

Following the directions with shaking hands, I open all three tests, pee on them, and set my alarm for five minutes. "This can't be right…" I whisper.

The little plastic sticks are neatly lined up on the counter and I stare at them. Each one with two bold pink lines.

I'm pregnant.

Mala does her best to keep up appearances and finally, we head back home. I want to curl up in bed and hold a pillow that smells like Cameron's woodsy, earthy scent and let my mind go blank. There are too many thoughts fighting with each other, each wanting attention and I don't want any of them.

"I have a wonderful doctor," Mala says kindly, "I can make you an appointment if you like."

"This… I…" There's a baby. I'm pregnant. With Cameron's child.

"It's okay, why don't you take some time and try to relax?" she says. "Are you going to tell Cameron tonight?"

"No!" I try to speak calmly. "Not when he's in danger. He needs to be able to concentrate. This is the final mission, you know that. Nothing can distract him right now."

She nods, giving me a gentle hug. "I get it. Do you want me to stay? Or, why don't you spend the night at my place? Catriona and Michael will give you a very up close and personal view of what's in your future."

"Thank you for offering your children up to me as an educational exercise," I force a laugh. "I just need some time to absorb this. I'll be okay."

"Fine, I'll get out of your way. But let me say one thing." She puts her hands on my shoulders. "You have a family here, people who care about you. Your child will have cousins and aunts and uncles, *sean-phàrantan*, grandparents who will dote on them. You're not alone."

Mala really is the best person ever.

Hugging her, I whisper, "Thank you. I needed to hear that."

Sitting in my chair in front of the open French doors in our bedroom, I close my eyes, feeling the light breeze over my face. Bad Cat's purring on my lap and he slaps a paw against my stomach.

"So, you know, too?" He looks up at me with his golden eyes, one at half-mast like a sneer.

I wish my mother was here. "Mama," I whisper, "I can make it right, now. I can make it up to you." There's a grim certainty that settles in my bones, like it's carved into my DNA.

It's time for my karmic payment. I won't live to see this baby grow up.

"Cameron's people are a strong family, mama. They'll take such good care of this child. I know I'm going to follow in your footsteps, I can feel it. But it will be all right. Cameron is going to be a wonderful father. They will all love this baby because he or she is Cameron's."

And so will I, I think, the tears finally freeing themselves.

CHAPTER TWENTY-EIGHT

In which there are so many secrets.

Morana...

Drifting through the next couple of days, I can't seem to focus on anything. Mala tactfully suggested we hold off on training until after I've seen the doctor.

Miss Kevin has taken to serving me ginger tea and crackers in the morning and it makes me feel vaguely paranoid. Have she and Bad Cat been talking?

"Hey, I haven't been in the pool house in forever." Mala's walking in the back garden with me, our security detail trailing behind us. When we get to the steamy, glassed enclosure she pulls me inside and shuts the door, leaving them to hover. "Did you know the roof in this place opens up?"

"Really?" I look up, endlessly amazed at all Cameron's little luxuries.

"I'm going to make you babysit the twins a lot," she says, pulling up her leggings so she can swish her feet in the water. "The pool at our place is one of those boring lap pools that Cormac put in for his workouts."

"That would be wonderful," I say, "I love kids. Growing up as an only child always made me wish I'd had siblings."

Looking around us, she leans closer. "Your appointment is set for tomorrow. If your guess about Dublin is correct, you're probably somewhere around eight weeks, so Dr. Greer says the ultrasound will give you a lot of information."

"I hate doing this without having Cameron there, but he's so deep in the mission. I think they're coming close to the final attack. Telling him this... risking the distraction? It feels wrong."

"Ordinarily, I'd try to convince you otherwise," Mala says, "but you're right. Cormac and Lachlan flew into Moscow this morning. They're ready for the push that drives Stepanov and your father out of their last stronghold there. They'll head for the compound outside of St. Petersburg and try to regain their forces. That's where Cameron and Dougal will be waiting. It's okay," she nudges me, "Cameron will be there for the next one."

"Thank you for coming with me. We have to find a reason for Natalia to not be there. She'll report this to Cameron, just out of spite."

"She really is unlikeable," Mala agrees. "Let me think on it."

Natalia is standing outside my bedroom door in the morning, dressed properly and swaying slightly.

"Are you all right?" I ask, concerned.

"I'm f-" Slapping her hand over her mouth, she races for my bathroom, vomiting noisily. It's all so reminiscent of the other day in the training room that for a moment, I'm wondering if *she's* pregnant. "I must have eaten something bad yesterday," she manages between clenched teeth.

"You need to go back to bed," I'd pat her back but she doesn't like the friendly, touchy type. "Don't worry, Mala and I are going out today, I'll ask her to double her guard."

"No, Mrs. MacTavish, that would be-"

I turn, waiting for her to finish throwing up. It's not helping my morning queasiness any, either. "Really, Natalia. Go to bed. The only people as vigilant as you are Mala's security."

When Mala shows up, right on time with a big, sunny smile, I eye her suspiciously.

"Natalia is horribly sick, she's thrown up half her body weight and everything but her toenails."

"That's terrible," she says without any change of expression.

"You graduated first in your class in the Spy Division, didn't you?"

"Well, the campus blew up, but up until that point, I was first in my class," she says modestly. "Now, we have things to do. Lovely to see you, Miss Kevin!"

Miss Kevin, who has been standing at the front door with her usual look of courteous inquiry, nods to me. "Have a pleasant lunch, Madame MacTavish."

"Um. Thank you, Miss Kevin, I won't be long."

Her left eye drops into the slightest of winks. Damn her. She's dangerous.

The old fear suddenly grips me again as Dr. Greer spreads the gel over my stomach for the ultrasound. This will be some cruel trick of fate. I won't really be pregnant.

My Russian stoicism takes over. What will be, will be.

Dr. Greer gently presses the doppler against my skin, sweeping it back and forth. "Ah, here we are." One hand still moving on my abdomen, he points with the other to the screen. "See there? There's your little one." He's making notes on size and measurements in a low voice to his nurse, and Mala grabs my hand.

"Oh, honey. You and Cameron are having a baby!" She hands me a tissue and I realize both of us are crying.

I *want* this baby. No matter what happens, I'll carry them safely until it's time to join their family.

"I'll keep you safe, *nemnogo lyubvi*, little love," I whisper.

Printing off a picture of my tiny baby, Dr. Greer hands it to me with a smile. "Now, let's talk a little about your family history," Dr. Greer asks.

And there goes my joy. "My mother died giving birth to me. She had placenta previa."

His pleasant expression doesn't change. "Well, that means we will keep a very close eye on you, but that is not a condition with a genetic predisposition. Try to remember that you'll be receiving the very best medical care, and keep your stress levels low, all right?"

Mala and I look at each other. *"Stress levels?"* she mouths at me. She squeezes my hands again. "Believe me, she'll be waited on hand and foot. You remember how Cormac was when I was pregnant?"

He swallows convulsively, "He was very protective."

"Some might say wildly over-the-top protective," Mala agrees, laughing. "Unfortunately, I think Cameron's going to be worse."

Dr. Greer's thin smile is not promising.

We're having a baby. I'm pregnant.

The thoughts cycle around each other in my head, making it impossible to do anything for the rest of the day.

"Madame Morana?"

I blink and realize I'm standing in the middle of the library, holding a book about 18th-century warfare. "Oh, hello," I say, clearing my throat.

"I thought you might like to have dinner out on the terrace? It's a warm evening."

"How long have you worked with the MacTavish family?"

If she finds my sudden change in topic unusual, she gives no sign of it. "Twenty years."

Frowning, I look more closely. "So, since you were ten?"

She chuckles politely but doesn't tell me her age. "I started in the Chieftain's household, and Cameron asked me to look after him about eight years ago."

"Have you always been a butler?"

Her eyes narrow, just slightly. Not threateningly. But the set of her jaw makes me think that no, Miss Kevin might have started in an entirely different line of work.

"How are ye' my sweet girl?" Cameron looks exhausted and there's a bandage on his shoulder.

"What happened? You just got over that bullet wound in your thigh!"

"I'm fine," he says dismissively, rubbing his eyes. "I may look like shite, but everything is going according to plan, better than I expected, in fact."

"Which means you should assume that something is about to go terribly wrong," I say.

"You and your bad luck theory," he groans, "and I'm telling you that we make our own luck, you and me. Look how everything is turnin' out after an unfortunate beginning involving a kidnapping-"

"And threatening to stick a hypodermic needle in my eye," I add pointedly.

"Let it go, lass! I'm thinkin' that now, we're a fortunate match. We like each other," he starts ticking off points on his fingers, "we're dynamite in bed, you're fit as feck, a bonnie lass, and-"

"Stop!" I'm laughing and he gives me a cheeky grin, looking so much better than he should, shirtless with all those perfectly sculpted muscles, even with that bandage and what looks like the beginning of a black eye. The tattoos on his chest and neck flex and move with him, like animated art. "I'm not sure what any of that last bit meant, but I think it was complementary." Sobering a bit, I look at his handsome, exhausted face. "Does it always have to be you?"

"What do ya' mean?"

"It's always you, first in the line of fire, leading the charge. I know you feel this responsibility, but..." I bite my lip, thinking of what to say that wouldn't sound needy and desperate. "You have people waiting for you at home, too," I finally say. "Maybe you don't always have to throw yourself into the face of the enemy."

"I canna ask my men to do something I'm not willing to do myself."

I snort inelegantly. "I'm certain they'll all quite clear that you're willing to jump in with both feet."

Did he pay any attention to what I was trying to say? Because he's staring at me, a sly grin stretching across his face. "You miss me, lass. Don't ya'?"

"That's what you got out of my persuasive argument?"

"What do you miss most, darlin'? My sparkling personality or my cock-"

"Hanging up!" I warn.

"Stop, stop," he's laughing, the conceited ass. "Don't hang up. I'm sorry that I had a bit of fun with ye'. But I *am* pleased that you're worried for me. I take every precaution I can, and my brothers are here, all in, just like me. I have a strong reason to live."

"What reason?"

This time, his smile is gentle. "You, love. I want to come home to ye' as much as you want me to, aye?"

Suddenly, I want to tell him about the baby, I want to see his expression. "Cameron, I…"

"Aye?"

"Nothing," I smile, "just happy to hear your brothers are there with you."

CHAPTER TWENTY-NINE

In which things go straight to hell.

Morana...

When I see Natalia waiting outside my bedroom door the next morning, I'm sincerely relieved to see that she looks much better. She may not like me, but what (Mala? Miss Kevin?) did to her yesterday was not kind.

"Good morning!" I force a smile, "Are you feeling better?"

"Yes, thank you, Mrs. MacTavish," she says between thin lips. There's something else in her eyes, some avaricious kind of glint that makes me uncomfortable.

She follows me closely down the stairs and I'm wondering if she wants to push me the rest of the way. There's a disturbing energy radiating off her today, more than her usual bland contempt.

That's when she presses a gun to my spine.

My first thought is, *not there, there's a baby not by the baby...*

Miss Kevin enters the hall, brow furrowed. "Is everything quite all right, Madame MacTavish?"

"Actually, Miss Kevin, we were hoping you could help us with a bit of a situation." Sven, Natalia's husband, is crowding the hall, along with three other men I've never seen before. "We'd like you to come with us, or we will shoot Morana Ivanova to pieces, right in front of you. That would be a dereliction of your duty, eh?"

Her eyes narrow in fury, but Miss Kevin nods.

"No, wait-" I look at Natalia, and my fury feels like a living thing, like it should burn her, just by touching me. "That's why it was so easy to disarm those men on the steps, they thought you were helping *them.* Look, I- I begged for your life then. It wasn't needed, but I did. Please leave Miss Kevin here. Please give me that-"

"I am happy to join you," Miss Kevin cuts me off.

"I promise I'll come with you quietly," I plow on, "just leave her here."

"Security cameras or not," Natalia whispers in my ear, making me shudder, "I will pistol-whip you if you don't shut up."

How can this be happening?

I feel the same way I did that morning at the Cathedral of Christ the Savior when Cameron came bursting into that room. My pieces of reality have shattered again and reformed themselves into a terrifying, unrecognizable new pattern.

Both Miss Kevin and I were handcuffed behind our backs, which cuts down on most of the moves Mala and Cameron had had time to teach me.

Cameron. This could destroy everything he's worked for, these past five years. All the people he's lost, his wounds, his scars. I can't let them ransom me. But Miss Kevin? How can I get her out of this?

We're at a private airfield, I recognize it. This is where we landed when Cameron kidnapped me. My Russian dourness appreciates the irony of being taken back from the same location.

Taking my chances, I beg Ivan. "Please leave Miss Kevin here. She's not involved in this, you don't-"

Natalia slaps me hard enough to knock me to the ground, and the look on her face tells me she's been *dying* to do that for a long time. Hauling me back up like a bag of dirt, she shoves me toward the waiting jet. "Get up those stairs or I'll drag you by your hair."

Miss Kevin is pushed up after me and as we enter the jet, she leans in close enough to whisper, "Have strength." Ivan pulls us apart again, putting her in the back bank of seats and me in the front.

I spent the five-hour flight to Moscow castigating myself. I should have known. I should have known what my father was doing, where the money came from that sent me to fine arts school, paid for my expensive clothes. Why didn't I ask more questions? Why didn't I *see* more?

The MacTavish Clan have spent years and countless resources tracking these evil bastards down and I was *right there.* Who knows how many girls I could have saved from the horrors of what Stepanov planned for them?

Ivan seats himself across from me, settling comfortably in the big leather seat. This must be a Stepnov jet, it's too ostentatious, even for my father. Everything is coated in gilt and the walls are wallpapered in a dark, flocked red, making me feel like I'm in the throat of a carnivorous beast.

"You've caused a great deal of trouble for yourself."

"How can you work for those scum?" I hiss, "They sell women and children. Do you partake? Are you a child rapist? You must be so proud."

He rewards me with a backhand on the opposite cheek of his wife's slap.

Nice, I think, a little dazed, *I'll have matching bruises.*

"You should learn to shut your mouth, though I suspect you'll have a cock stuffed in it for the rest of your miserable life." Ivan's got that bland, blond handsomeness that is stereotypical Norwegian, but right now he looks like a troll to me, something misshapen and hideous, like his soul.

"Why did you take Miss Kevin?" I persist.

"She would have raised the alarm in less than an hour if she wasn't clear on your whereabouts. Did you think she was just a butler?" He laughed at me.

"Miss Kevin is an excellent butler!" I snap. Why that is what offends me the most, I don't know, but it does.

He ignores me, of course. "The MacTavish Mafia has caused endless problems for the Bratva, but that should end soon. You had better pray that they think you are as valuable as you assume."

Chuckling mirthlessly, I shake my head. "I don't think that at all, I suspect your hopes are unrealistic. I was kidnapped as a hostage, remember? Just to keep Stepanov from marrying me."

He leans forward, hands on his thighs. His eyes are an icy blue, a chilling oscillation of hate, cruelty, and malice. "You'd better pray to all your Russian gods that you're wrong. It can always be so much worse than you could imagine."

My handcuffs were beginning to cut into my wrists as they hauled me off the jet, but the SUV waiting for us was smaller, so Miss Kevin and I were shoved in the back together.

"Are you all right?" she barely whispered, but Natalia heard her, whipping around from the front seat to punch her in the face. Miss Kevin calmly turns her head, spitting the blood flowing from her split lip onto the window.

Pressing my knee against hers, the only part I could reach, I gave her a small smile, and she nodded back. I should feel guilty that this woman's been dragged into my mess - and I am - but I'm so grateful she's here with me.

My heart sinks the deeper we drive into Moscow. The parks and beautiful buildings slowly disappear, the houses smaller and more poorly kept, and then we're deep into the industrial area in the Tverskoy District. It looks like Cameron didn't flush out all the Stepanov rat holes. The car comes to a stop near a warehouse next to the train tracks, and we're hauled inside. Men are shouting at each other and I catch just enough to know things are not going as planned.

Stifling a smile, I feel a wave of love sweep over me for Cameron. He has been relentless, driving these lowest of men to their bloody finish. I may not be there to see it, but at this moment, I cannot be happier.

In the confusion, Miss Kevin has been inching toward me and I catch her looking at all the exits. That's right, Mala taught me. Always look for your way out.

The arguing is reaching some sort of crescendo and Ivan turns back to us. "Enough of this shit!" He looks at me. "Natalia, put her on the train." His gun comes up and I scream, trying to lunge at him. "You, Miss Kevin, are no longer useful."

The gun goes off and I see her fall to the grimy concrete floor. I kick and thrash violently, ignoring Natalia's curses and slaps as she drags me out the door. As we approach the open doors of the train car I can hear the terrified sobbing of human souls inside. An electric-white flash of light bolts through my skull as the agonizing pain hits from Natalia's gun slamming into the back of my head. Then, my eyes go as dark as the interior of the train.

CHAPTER THIRTY

In which things can always get worse. And they do.

Morana...

I've seen my father do terrible things. Unspeakable things.

Sitting in the dark, rattled around by the movement of the train cars and hearing the subdued sobbing and moaning around me, I wonder when he went from simply being evil to an utter stain on humanity, a scourge. How could any human being see what's happened here and feel anything other than horror? The girl chained next to me can't be older than sixteen, and her pinched face and painfully thin body make me wonder if this is her first trip to hell. Maybe she's been there before. Her torn slip doesn't cover much, so I pull off my sweater.

"Here, hold your arms up," I show her the sweater, but she stares at me blankly. "You'll be warmer in this, okay? Can I help you put it on?"

Slowly, her skinny arms rise and I gently put the sweater over her head, helping her find the arm holes. Her legs curl in and I try not to cringe when I see the blood and bruising around her ankle shackle.

"I'm Morana, what's your name?" I try to get her to talk, though the empty stare never leaves her eyes. She smooths her hand over the sweater, so I hope it's a good sign.

A sharp chuckle breaks the silence. "Very sweet."

The woman across from me looks closer to my age though, at twenty, I'm pretty sure I'm the oldest one here.

"You should have kept it," she says, "it's going to get cold tonight." Stretching out her legs, I see her slight wince when the movement pulls on her ankle cuff.

"How long have you been on this train?"

She shrugs, "Two days, maybe three. They drug us when we come close to civilization." She's speaking Russian, but with an accent.

"You're from Ukraine?" I ask.

"Yes, the war hasn't slowed down the stealing of women," she said bitterly.

Squinting in the dark, I can see the train car is full of girls, maybe fifty in total. We're all chained to the wall. The smell is my first clue that there are no toilets, no food, no water. The stench of ripe, unwashed bodies is overwhelming. There's a low soundtrack of suffering; soft weeping, and moans as the girls change positions and their chains rattle.

Closing my eyes, I try to track where we might be going. They took me to Moscow.

Miss Kevin! Is she alive? Please let her be alive. "Can you tell me how long it's been since they threw me in here?"

"What does it matter?"

"I'm trying to figure out where they're taking us."

Two of the others start sobbing.

The girl across from me snaps, "Shut up. This is bad enough, don't upset them more."

"What did I say?"

Lowering her voice, she leans closer. "They told us that where they're taking us, we'll never leave there alive."

My father needs to die. Stepanov should be torn apart in a thousand pieces. If I'm given the gift of any time left on this earth, I'll use it to kill them both.

After another hour or so, the train jerks to the left, slowing down slightly and changing direction. I can smell the slight tinge of salt. We're heading toward the ocean. This could be their facility near Sosnovy Bor. If that's the case, Cameron may know where I'm going.

A huge surge of homesickness hits me. I miss our house. Bad Cat. I miss my husband with his forest-green eyes and his filthy mouth. I look down at my wedding ring and realize it's gone. There's a long scrape on my finger as if someone impatiently ripped it off. That's the thing that finally makes me cry, smothering my sobs so I don't make it worse for the others.

Cameron...

I'm watching the screen as the drone silently crisscrosses the countryside over the railroad tracks.

"How close?"

Dougal folds his arms, checking the readout. "Twenty minutes. The heat signatures are clustered heavily on two of the train cars, I'm guessing around a hundred bodies or so. The rest are spread out, about twenty guards in total." He checks his watch. "They'll enter the zone where there's no cell signal in twelve minutes. We'll have a jammer activated for the radio communication in the engine car at fifteen minutes exactly."

"I knew ye' were the smartest of us," I compliment him.

Dougal laughs. "Ye' called me a lavvy-heided wankstain yesterday."

"It was a heat of the moment thing," I defend myself.

"Uh-huh." Turning to our men, he shouts, "Shut yer syphilis-ridden herpes holes, ya' cunts! The boss is talking!"

Pinching the bridge of my nose, I take a deep breath. "Thank you, brother, so helpful."

"You're welcome," he smiles supportively.

"Clan," I say, "in precisely eighteen minutes we're stopping and boarding this train. It is crucial that there is no outward damage to alert those cum-splats that anything is amiss. We jump in, get the women out, and load that fucker up with the C4. We have precisely six minutes to do this. The engineer has orders to communicate with the compound every thirty minutes. Sync your watches now."

All fifty men and women lift their arms and click their timepieces in unison. These are good people.

While the Morozov and Turgenev Bratvas have sent ground support for the last six skirmishes as we drove Stepanov to his eventual end, I wanted MacTavish Clan members for the last. They deserve to see the bloody and fiery end after all our organization has given. O'Rourke never offered any of his people and I'm not sure I would have trusted them. In the end, O'Rourke is only for himself.

None of this might have happened, though, without my wife. No one had the location of Stepanov's biggest compound and central "processing" facility for his human cargo, not even O'Rourke.

Checking my watch again, I want to call her. Afterwards. I'll have more to tell her then. Still, there's an insistent nudge in the base of my spine, wanting to call her. Setting it aside, I take a deep breath. Timing has never been more important.

Concentrate, you arse.

Precisely eighteen minutes later, the train rounds the tracks a quarter mile from where I have two huge, military-grade Humvees parked across the track. It will take a quarter mile's distance for the engineer to slam on the brakes and stop in time to avoid a collision.

"Radio signal jammer's up," Dougal announces as the other

vehicles close in on the train. We board the train before it's fully stopped and shoot everyone holding a gun, ten team members are already guarding the two cars with the captives, making sure Ivanov's guard can't shoot them, which is standard evil bastard protocol.

"How are we doing?" I query into my headset, hearing the different teams confirm their location. Then Dougal's voice interrupts.

"Brother, come to car two."

"What's up?"

His voice is urgent, "Just come here. Now."

Tearing through the cars, I kick aside the bodies of the Ivanov soldiers. Bursting into Dougal's train car, I squint in the low light.

"What is-?"

He's holding a woman, our medic rapidly pressing bandages on her bleeding stomach.

It's my Morana.

My wife, bleeding out on the filthy floor, her leg still in shackles.

CHAPTER THIRTY-ONE

In which the worst place to find your wife is on a filthy train car with a bullet wound.

Morana...

When I was ten, the Ivanov Bratva joined two other families from the Moscow Six for a train ride to St. Petersburg to meet with the major Bratvas there. My father complained bitterly about the stupid sentimentality of such a trip, how a plane or helicopter ride would be so much faster. He was especially irritated that he was expected to bring me since the other Pakhans brought their children.

The only drama was a herd of cows casually grazing along the train tracks, and the locomotive had to stop to shoo them away. I remember how long it took for the train to come to a stop. My father and a couple of the other less civilized men took turns shooting the cows as the train crew struggled to clear the tracks.

So, when we all go sprawling as the train jolts violently, I know the high-pitched screech of the brakes on the rails can only mean an emergency stop. Which, *Bozhe pozhaluysta,* please God, could mean Cameron found us. Found me.

I hold onto the girl I'd given my sweater when she slides into me, whimpering softly. "It's okay," I tell her, hoping she speaks Russian, "It will be all right." This could be a lie, but I want to believe, I need to believe that this isn't how the story ends for us all.

When the door is kicked open, the girls all scream, and my heart sinks as I recognize him; Kirill is one of the Ivanov brigadiers, he's an evil pig and he's perfect for this job. Torturing and terrifying young girls must be a dream for him.

His gun is out, he's searching the car and I know he's looking for me. I can't let him start shooting randomly, I know he won't stop. He probably has orders to kill all the girls.

"Hey, Kirill Galkin, *svoloch',* you bastard!" I stand up so he can see me and the girl in my sweater pulls on my shirt, trying to make me sit down. His eyes are jittering back and forth and his hand holding the gun is shaking.

Kirill's scared. That can only mean...

"It's over, Kirill Galkin! If you hurt any of these girls, they will torture you. The MacTavish Mafia is very creative." He's staring at me, lips peeled back in a snarl. "Drop the gun, don't make it worse."

There are shouts behind him, boots pounding down the narrow hall.

So close they're so close.

This seems to galvanize him and he lifts his gun, pointing it in my direction. "I have my orders," he rasps, "you'll not leave this train car alive Morana Ivanova, *shlyukha,* you whore!"

He's going to shoot me. That's okay. Better me than them. But then his gun barrel wavers and he's aiming at the Sweater Girl and I shout, "I'm over here, you fuck! I knew your aim was shit but this is-"

I thought it would hurt worse.

It feels like a giant fist punches me in the chest, throwing me backward. I hear screaming and it's not mine because I can't breathe and there's blood and that is mine. It's bubbling from my stomach like a fountain and I press my hands on it trying to make it go away.

"Oh, fuck."

I know that voice. Dougal's hands are on my face and he's ripped off his jacket to put it under my head.

"Get the medic!"

The Sweater Girl is holding my hand, but I'm getting cold and it's hard to feel her.

This is the true curse of the Ivanovs. That finally, when I've found love, when I'm going to be a mother, I'm going to die on this train filled with my father's other victims. But maybe that will finally make it right.

"My sweet girl what- oh, love…" Cameron is hovering over me, cupping my face.

"Hey…" I smile as he kisses my forehead, my lips. A woman is pushing him aside and her capable hands are on my stomach, pressing down and it burns so much. Now the pain comes slamming down on me and I wail before I can stop it.

Now, I remember. "Baby…" I groan. Cameron shakes his head, confused, his eyes wet.

"Ma'am, are you pregnant?" the woman interrupts.

"Yes." It's too soon. I knew I would die but the baby's not ready. "Too soon…" Her hands are a blur and Cameron is shouting something. I close my eyes. Just for a minute.

Cameron…

Morana has been adamant about the karmic bad luck that she thinks follows her like a black cloud. I always dismissed it as part of her superstitious Russian roots. But how is she lying on the filthy floor of this train car? Why isn't she safe at home?

A baby. We're having a *baby?*

"Boss, we are taking your wife out of this train car," Davina, our medic, shouts in my ear. "I need to know you are listening to me right now."

Everything that faded into gray around us suddenly slams back into full-color intensity and I nod, rising as they lift Morana onto a makeshift stretcher. Like muscle memory, I look down at my watch. Sixty seconds behind schedule. The girls are all safely loaded in the vehicles. Then everything about the mission is gone and my wife is the only thing that matters.

"Brother, the C4 is loaded," Dougal's gripping my shoulder as we race for the helicopter. "I'll see to this. You go with your wife."

Years of planning and fighting to end the last strain of the disease that was the Yakuza and Bratva who kidnapped my sister and my little cousins. I've visualized pushing the button on those explosives maybe a thousand times since we made this plan. Now all the details are hazy and indistinct, the sight of my pale Morana, heaving for breath is the only thing I can see.

"Go." I choke out the words, "Thank you."

Slapping my arm, he nods. "Go take care of yer wife, arsehole. I got this."

I hear the train start up again as Morana is secured, but I don't look back. We're up in the air and speeding toward St. Petersburg and I whisper like a prayer, "You're all right. The baby is fine. I love you, wife."

CHAPTER THIRTY-TWO

In which there are hospital rooms. And long-awaited justice

Cameron…

My headphones crackle and I hear Cormac's voice. "Brother, we've got a problem. Stepanov had people in your circle, the Norwegian couple. They took Morana and Miss Kevin to Moscow. I just got a call from Miss Kevin, they shot her and left her for dead, she doesn't know where Morana-"

"She's with me," I interrupt. "They put her on the train, chained like a dog. One of Ivanov's men shot her in the stomach."

"Shite. Brother…" I hear his sorrow for me. "Is she alive?"

"Aye, we're flyin' her into St. Petersburg."

"Take her to the Euromed Private Hospital, I'll call ahead and have the trauma surgeon waiting for her. He's one of the best."

"She's pregnant." My voice breaks.

"Ya' didn't know?"

"No. I think… she wanted to tell me last night but she stopped." I look down at my wife, brushing her bloodied hair back from her face. Davina puts an oxygen mask over her mouth and checks her pulse.

"It's thready, boss, but it's there."

Cormac's talking and it takes me a minute to focus. "I'm patching in Dr. Blanchet, stay off the line and let him talk to Davina. We'll be there as quickly as we can."

"Find Natalia and Sven first," I snarl. "They do not leave this country alive."

"Aye. I understand," he says, "be strong."

We land directly on top of the hospital, and the trauma team is waiting, feet braced against the turbulence from the helicopter. I keep my hand on Morana's leg as they lift her out and take her hand again as we race through the halls. Dr. Blanchet is already ordering multiple pints of blood. As the operating room door swings open, he steps in front of me.

"I am aware of the importance of these two precious lives," he says steadily. He's a brave man because my gun is already halfway out of my holster. "Are you capable of standing in the back and not approaching under any circumstances? You could kill your wife if you interfere. Do you understand me, Mr. MacTavish?"

My gun is back in my holster. "Aye," I agree, "focus on my wife. I won't make a sound."

Davina is hastily gowned and gloved up as she goes over the wound with the doctor. "Exit wound in the back," she murmurs, helping to roll Morana gently. A moan comes from her and I clench my fists.

Steady. You do not move a muscle.

"... a lot of blood..."

"...nicked an artery..."

"...pregnant..."

Dr. Blanchet looks up, "How far along is she, Mr. MacTavish?"

My throat's tight. "I don't know."

When the doctor steps back from the table, he looks deeply relieved as he pulls off his mask. "Your wife is going to be all right."

"The baby?" I manage to choke out.

He gives me a sympathetic smile, "I'll need to do an ultrasound, but she's stabilized for now. There's no indication of miscarriage. The bullet entry and exit were nowhere near the uterus. Why don't you come sit with her in her room?"

Nodding firmly, I try to blink away the moisture. "Aye. Thank you."

The room is darkened and the only light comes from the glow of all the machines around her. Dr. Blanchet murmurs something about "Overkill…" to Davina, but she shakes her head.

"Trust me doc, you should bring in every possible thing that can monitor Mrs. MacTavish's health. It will guarantee the continued good health of yourself."

It's just the two of us now, my wife and me. Kissing her hand, I watch her pale face. "I'm sorry love, I'm sorry I didn't replace Natalia the instant we talked about her, if I had taken ten goddamn minutes to switch her out, you wouldn't have been in danger."

Her chest rises and falls with her breath, but the movement is slight, it's too shallow.

"You wanted to tell me about the baby, didn't you?" Giving a wet chuckle, I kiss her hand again. "I'm thinkin' back and we had that moment in Dublin. The back seat? It's a better story to tell our kiddos than our first wedding, aye?" Smoothing my hand over her arm. "Maybe not the specifics of the night, but… All the girls from the train are safe, love. Every one of them. I know that will be the second thing you'll want to know, after the baby. The wee one is fine."

With a sigh, I kiss her again. "Sleep, *leannan, a ghràidh,* sweetheart, my love."

Dougal...

The train starts up and I check the AI program that will mimic the engineer's voice for the check-in. How could those arrogant pricks not have the slightest suspicion, even though they're barricaded in their last safe place?

Stepanov's compound is huge, with fifteen-foot steel reinforced walls. There's a closed port that's impossible to approach via the waterway without instantly givin' away our position. But those stupid dug licking pish were so confident about their slave trains that loading up the cars with C4 was the easiest thing.

There's a desire in me to call Stepanov, and tell him his arse is about to blow sky high and takin' his men and legacy with him. It feels anticlimactic after the years we've put into destroying this bastard. I thought my brothers would be with me...

Turning to the men and women who joined us on this mission, I raise the detonator like a toast. Checking my watch, I count it down.

"Three... two..."

"The train is in the compound," Hamish reports gleefully.

"Tongue ma fart-box, ya fuckin' walloper!" I shout.

And press the button on the detonator.

Cameron...

I don't know how long it's been, but when I look up, all three of my brothers are crowded into the doorway and if I had been in a laughing mood, I'd be howlin' right now. They look fecking ridiculous, all trying to squeeze through first.

"At least you washed all the blood off," I murmur.

"How is she?" Lachlan is trying to whisper, which for him is just under a shout.

"Stable," I say gratefully, running my hands through my hair. "And pregnant. Eight weeks or so, the doc thinks."

"Well done, brother!" Cormac grips my shoulder with a grin. "Good news all around today, then."

"Tell me everything," I whisper eagerly.

"I wanna know who the feck determined just how much C4 we were gonna need," Dougal hisses. "Look at my face!"

Cormac and Lachlan are nearly choking, trying to keep from laughing and disturbing my wife's rest.

Dougal looks rough. The force of the blast knocked trees flat, and disintegrated structures and roads for one and a half kilometers around the compound. Even though our team was over three kilometers away, one side of his face was a wee bit crispy.

"We flew over the compound," Lachlan says gleefully, "and there's nothin' standing. Not one brick attached to another. The train and vehicles in the compound are chunks of twisted metal. Shite, I wish we could have seen Stepnov's expression!"

"What matters here is that it's done," Cormac says soberly.

"Tell me Natalia and Sven are dead," I say.

"You'll enjoy this. They were all tucked up snug in the compound with the others. We got some mighty clear images of them both," he grins.

"Miss Kevin? What happened there?" Dougal asks. When I poached her from our parents, he was furious that he didn't think of it first, the idiot. I think he's a bit sweet on her.

"That woman is amazing," Cormac says, shaking his head, "they took them both because they knew Miss Kevin would raise the alarm if Morana went missing. When they put yer wife on the train in Moscow, they shot Miss Kevin, they got her shoulder instead of her heart. Thank the Lord for a shite aim."

"Aye," they all nod fervently.

"When she regained consciousness, she dragged herself out of the worst slum in Moscow - still handcuffed - and convinced the first person she found to let her use their cell phone. And hear this; she knew all our numbers. By heart."

"Mighty good luck that you and Lachlan were still in Moscow," Dougal says in relief.

"She's patched up in one of our safe houses," Cormac continues, "she'll fly home in the morning."

"I can take her on my jet," Dougal offers a little too eagerly.

Before my brothers can give him a round of shite, I see Morana's eyelashes flutter. "Get the feck out." They slip out the door, closing it behind them.

Her brows draw together before she forces her eyes open, blinking slowly, widening when they land on me.

"Baby…" she's got a croaky little voice and I put her hand on my cheek.

"The baby's fine, love. Eight weeks along, the doctor said."

"Yes," she whispers, "Dublin."

I chuckle quietly. "Aye."

"Girls?" I hear one of the machines that goes 'ping' every few minutes start pinging more quickly.

"Shhh, they're all safe," I say hastily, "I swear it. Take a couple of deep breaths for me?"

She tries and winces. "Hurts."

Leaning in, I kiss her forehead, her cheekbones, and her lips. "The doctor's gonna come in ragin' in just a second and there's gonna be a lot of commotion. So let me say this now. *Tha gaol agam ort. YA tebya lyublyu.* In Gaelic and Russian and every language, I love you."

Her eyes turn the deepest shade of violet, the color of the tiny flowers in the sun and she is... pure light. "I love you too. So much."

And then the doctor comes racin' in and it's hoaching crowded.

CHAPTER THIRTY-THREE

In which Cameron locks down The Husband of the Year Award.

Morana...

Ten days later, long after Dr. Blanchet pronounces me safe to travel, Cameron finally sets me free from the hospital. Most of the staff genuinely looks sad to see us go, which would be sweet except for the fact that I know he hired a full catering staff to feed everyone even remotely connected to my care, twenty-four hours a day. If I were waving goodbye to a limitless supply of caviar, *pirozhki*, and *shashlik*, I'd be sad, too.

After carrying me to the car despite my protests, he carefully puts on my seatbelt before climbing in the back with me, and we pull out of the hospital parking lot with two SUVs in front of us and two behind. Very subtle.

Hamish gives me a cheeky wink from the front.

"Looking fine, ma'am."

"Thank you Hamish, but can't you call me Morana?"

"Not if I want to keep my eyes," he says pleasantly.

"Cameron..." I rest my head on his shoulder, "he helped save my life. Don't you think we could be on a first-name basis?"

He kisses me tenderly on the forehead. "No."

When we pull up in front of the magnificent Hermitage Museum, I look at him with a little frown. "We have time to sightsee? Not that I am complaining," I add hastily, "this is my favorite museum in the entire world."

"I know," he smiles as he gets out of the car, "you told me once."

"You remembered that?" I gasp. We'd talked about so many things during our Facetime sessions when he was away, hunting my father and Stepanov. I didn't realize he'd been paying such close attention.

Lifting me out of the car and into a wheelchair despite my protests, he kisses me gently. "I remember everything you told me."

This entire section of the massive museum is closed, which makes no sense. This is one of the most legendary art museums in the world, and tourists are always crowding the halls. But I can hear Cameron's dress shoes click on the marble flooring in the empty space as we enter the Large Italian Skylight Room.

"And this is my favorite section!" I gasp, eagerly looking around me. "See *Thatched Cottages*, the one there on the left? That's a Van Gogh, and there's *The Woman Holding Fruit* by Paul Gaugin..."

Cameron finally comes to a stop in front of my most beloved painting here, *The Madonna Litta.*

My Russian stoicism deserts me as rapturous tears come to my eyes. I stand, ignoring his anxious grip on my arm. "This was painted by Leonardo da Vinci. See the tenderness of the mother, feeding her baby? The curve of her head and the light on her face as she looks down at her little one?"

His arm comes around me, cradling me and perhaps holding me up just a bit as we stand together, looking at the beauty of this painting in silence.

"I'd always pictured my mother and me like this painting, if she'd lived, but now when I look at it, I see myself with our child," I whisper.

Leading me over to a nearby bench, he kneels, kissing my ring finger. The scrape from where they tore it off me is nearly healed by now.

"I'm sorry they took the ring," I say sadly.

"It's all right. It's just a ring," he kisses my finger again. "But I would like to do this again, properly."

"We've already been married three times," I laugh quietly.

"Let's start with a proper proposal, aye? I would very much like to marry you." He kisses my hand with a gentleness that makes me weak. This hard, harsh man who is capable of unspeakable violence, yet at this moment can show such tenderness.

"I'm a clever man," he continues, "so I was certain I'd find something romantic to say to you, something to curl your toes and make you throw your arms around me saying 'Yes, yes!' But instead, I see a woman who I likely don't deserve, and... you would likely agree. I also see the mother of my child and now, like what you've seen in this painting, I have a vision, too of the three of us together. Morana MacTavish, would you marry me?"

He holds up a glimmering diamond ring with a huge center stone and a scattering of violet-colored stones around it.

"Of course!" I sob, "Of course I would!"

Cameron grins, looking relieved as if my answer was ever in question and he slips the ring on my finger. "It's not too harsh on your sore finger?"

"No, *lyubov'*, love. It's perfect." When he helps me to my feet, I see that a beaming, expensively suited man has entered the hall with Hamish.

"Cameron Cian MacTavish, Morana Ivanova MacTavish, I am Aleksey Komarov, Governor of St. Petersburg. It would be my honor to re-marry you and your husband today."

I look down at the pretty white dress Cameron helped me into this morning. That makes sense. "Your Excellency Aleksey Komarov, it would be a great favor to us both. We are honored."

He conducts the service in a mix of Russian and English, and when we both say "I do," he nods as if nothing could be better than this moment.

And I agree with him.

CHAPTER THIRTY-FOUR

In which life is like Downton Abbey, but with semi-automatic weapons.

Morana...

I don't think even Beyonce has an entourage this outrageous.

"Get the wheelchair out," Cameron barks into the phone, "I want it waiting when we pull up."

"Please *lyubov'*, love," I groan, "I don't need a wheelchair. I didn't lose function in my legs."

"You're unsteady on your feet," he frets, "let's just use the wheelchair for right now, aye? I've already had the staff renovate one of the downstairs rooms into a bedroom for you right now so you don't have to climb the stairs."

"I am not an invalid!"

My protests fall on deaf ears, of course. We pull into the driveway and... oh, he has the entire staff on the front stairs? This is so ridiculous!

"This *is* like Downton Abbey but with guns," I groan.

"Bollocks!" Cameron scoffs, "We're nothing like that English poncery."

We pull up to the front steps, trailed by two SUVs, one is carrying a disgruntled Dr. Blanchet, who was informed that he would be spending a week at our home as an 'honored guest,' whether he wanted to or not. I'm hoping to convince Cameron that he's turned into a tall, gorgeous bag of crazy and he's got to calm down. He's already forced poor Dr. Greer to be waiting for us so he can give me an immediate examination.

Will he get even more unhinged as the pregnancy progresses? Is that even possible?

Cameron lifts me out of the car and into the wheelchair. This is ridiculous. He proudly pushes me up to the line of household employees.

Smiling weakly and greeting each person, I'm surprised at how warmly they're responding to me. It feels sincere, like they might be happy that I'm alive. Miss Kevin is standing at the end, wearing her butler's uniform, her arm in a discreet sling, and holding Bad Cat, who is glaring at me.

Before my obsessed husband can stop me, I rise from the wheelchair and get as close as I dare. "I really want to hug you right now and thank you for saving my life, Miss Kevin," I whisper. "I recognize this would be inappropriate, but... you nearly gave your life for me. I will never be able to thank you."

She very gingerly shakes my hand. "It was my pleasure. Welcome home, Madame Morana." I notice the slightest sheen of emotion in her warm brown eyes. Gently squeezing her hand, I sit back down as she puts Bad Cat on my lap.

When I see the room Cameron has set up for me, I burst out laughing, which I then immediately regret. Holding a hand over my bullet wound, I view what looks like a complete surgical suite.

"Am I pregnant or slowly dying from a hideous, lingering disease?" I ask.

"I want to make sure we're prepared for anything," he says stubbornly.

"Uh-huh... I'm not sleeping in here. This is so depressing."

"Mrs. MacTavish, please do get on the bed for an examination, at least." Dr. Greer puts a hospital gown on the bed, smiling hopefully. "Your husband has indicated that I am not allowed to leave before I give you a complete workup."

Recognizing that two highly regarded physicians will not be allowed to leave this house until my husband's wildly overprotective mania is satisfied, I sigh sadly.

"I just got out of the hospital," I mumble.

Cameron shuts the door and helps me change into the gown.

"I've already spoken with Dr. Blanchet-"

"Your fellow captive?" I ask, glaring up at a completely unrepentant Cameron.

"-my colleague who updated me on your bullet wound," Dr. Greer continues, unperturbed, "and we went over the x-rays and recovery plan. I feel very confident that the wound will not impact the pregnancy, but let's have a look."

After a basic exam, which takes twice as long because my enormous husband insists on looming over Dr. Greer like a Scottish Yeti, he pulls over the ultrasound machine. "Let's check on your little one."

Cameron sits next to me, holding my hand. "I'm sorry I wasn't here for the first one," he whispers.

"You had a lot going on," I say, kissing his chin, the only part of him I can reach.

My atavistic fear of bad luck rises again. What if they're wrong? What if the bullet took our baby?

Dr. Greer manipulates the Doppler over my abdomen. "Sorry..." he murmurs when I wince when he presses down.

"It's fine, do what you need to."

"Ah, there we are." He points to the screen, "See there?"

There's *nemnogo lyubvi,* my little love, pulsing like a star.

My husband's expression is a mix of hope, joy, shock,

excitement, and a few other emotions cycle over that I don't understand.

"Are you happy?" I ask nervously.

"My wife, I... We're going to have a baby!" Cameron announces joyfully, as if this is the first time we've all heard of it.

"Yes, this is true," I'm laughing and maybe crying a bit but he's so happy. The man who coldly kidnapped me from the church in Moscow is gone forever. This is the husband I married in Ireland, in Russia. *My* husband.

"How are you feeling, dear?"

The Lady Elspeth seats herself next to me on the enormous stone terrace outside of the MacTavish mansion. We're watching the men playing some odd permutation of football with the twins riding piggyback on Cormac and Cameron.

"I'm very well, thank you, ma'am. But perhaps you could convince your son to stop treating me like I'm going to shatter like a crystal goblet if he lets me take a single step by myself?"

She gave an elegant chuckle, watching the action on the lawn.

"You know, some of the past MacTavish matriarchs would retire to the Dowager House-" she nodded toward the beautiful replica of the main house, but about the fourth the size, across the gardens. "To enjoy the rest of their pregnancy without their men stomping through their relaxation. That seems going a bit too far as I see it, but we can always threaten your husband if he doesn't find a way to calm down."

"I'm willing to consider it," I say fervently.

"Did he truly build you a complete surgical suite at the house?"

Nodding, I take a sip of my juice. "I'm certain they could perform open-heart surgery there. I wouldn't mind keeping it for all the inevitable skirmishes these men get into. I just don't want to be in there. It's depressing."

"Fortunately, the Clan's activity is primarily white collar, financial, banking, money laundering, and the like," she says. "The greatest danger seems to come from bar fights in one of our many clubs."

Sorcha skips over to the football melee, joining in. I watch her pale face flush with laughter as she darts back and forth like a dragonfly.

"Maybe now that the Stepanov and Ivanov Bratvas no longer exist, it will be... easier for Sorcha? I don't presume to understand anything about what she went through."

Lady Elspeth lightly pats my hand. It's as shocking as if she's reached over and grabbed me in a bear hug. "You understand quite a bit, I suspect. My daughter has not left these grounds since Cormac brought her home. But now? Perhaps anything is possible."

We sit and sip our drinks like proper ladies, watching the family laugh and shout, getting covered in mud.

EPILOGUE

In which we meet new friends and old enemies.

Four months later...

Cameron...

"To the MacTavish Clan!" Da' starts the toast.

"To new beginnings!" says Cormac.

"To our child!" I shout gleefully.

"To owning this new pub, which is mighty braw!" Dougal slams back his shot.

"What does braw mean?" Morana whispers.

"It means mighty fine or great," I kiss her forehead.

"And here's to this bottle of finely aged forty-year-old whiskey and may it never run dry!" Lachlan finishes the round.

The O'Rourke Distillery is changing hands from Nolan to the MacTavish Clan under my ownership. As per our agreement, he's gained control over all the water and overland shipping routes once owned by the Stepanov and Ivanov Bratvas. Still, he insisted on meeting tonight to give us what he said was, 'A small gift in celebration of our victory.'

"This is quite a gift," Morana gasps. "Isn't this one of the oldest distilleries in Ireland? This is a legendary building!"

"Ah, you were listening that night when we talked about the distillery's history," he taps the tip of her nose and I'm seconds away from snapping that finger from his hand... if she doesn't bite it off first.

"Why would you gift us with something so treasured?" I ask, "I know how important this distillery is to you, to own a piece of Irish history."

"I find myself…" O'Rourke looks around the beautiful, airy dining room. It's closed tonight for our private party. "…dissatisfied. The fire and subsequent repairs were tedious. While it might appear to be the same, it is not."

He gives us a huge smile, showing all those white teeth, like a shark. "I thought to myself, what would be an appropriate gift for such a valiant family? Not only have you given me access to Russian properties that I find highly useful, you also rid the world of more trafficking vermin." The last part was clearly an afterthought from him, but I'll take it.

"What could be more magnificently Scottish than a premium whiskey distillery? After all, the only difference between the Scots and Irish love of whiskey is taking out that 'e' in the word. You Scots, so frugal even with your spelling," he chuckles.

"Oh, I always wondered about that," Mala murmurs, "why it's 'whiskey' in Ireland and 'whisky' in Scotland."

"That, I cannot answer, but you can choose to spell this fermented magnificence in any way that pleases you," O'Rourke says, presenting the deed with great ceremony to me.

"Then we'll celebrate with enthusiasm and sincere appreciation," I say. "Because of our alliances with the Morozov and Turgenev Bratvas in St. Petersburg, I did place a call to their partner here in Ireland as a courtesy to let them know we'd be doing business in Dublin. It doesn't step on any toes, but it is important to observe the boundary issue."

"Oh?" Morana asks, "Who is that?"

"Patrick and Aisling Doyle. The Doyle Clan is growing into quite a powerful organization here in Ireland."

"You must surely be joking."

I turn to find a tall, attractive couple standing behind us, the man's only in his late thirties but already sporting a full head of silver hair. The fiery-looking woman next to him with blazing green eyes might be the reason for the early gray.

"Patrick and Aisling?" I hold out my hand. "A pleasure to meet ya'. Maksim and Yuri Morozov have hailed you as one of the finest things to escape from Russia."

Patrick chuckled, almost unwillingly, but took my hand in a firm shake. "My beautiful wife Aisling, who is like to take a corkscrew and stab Nolan O'Rourke in the heart in just a moment."

"Aye…" I slip my arm around my wife's waist, "This my lovely bride Morana, and please, no violence in front of the pregnant lady."

Looking back, I see that Nolan hasn't gotten up from his chair, simply lounging with a gloating expression on his unnaturally young face.

"We wanted to introduce ourselves and break bread together, as we will be doing business here in Dublin. We would, of course, not cross yer' boundaries, but there might be room for collaboration."

"The Morozov brothers speak highly of ye' as well, Cameron. Tell me, what's yer business here?" Patrick asks, keeping a firm grip on his wife's arm.

Spreading my arms wide, I announce, "The new MacTavish Whisky Distillery."

Patrick looks horrified, as if he'd seen the Lost Ark of the Covenant and his face was about to melt off.

"Just kidding," I chuckle. "We're bringing back the original name the distillery had for it's first 145 years, The Killaney Distillery."

"That bastard gave ye' the *distillery?*" he grits out.

"Aye?" Looking between them, I can tell this is not good news.

"*Mo stór,* my darling," Aisling says, patting his chest. "It's all right. This is good. As long as it's not O'Rourke's."

"I can tell there's a long story there and one I'm eager to hear-"

"Me, too," Morana interrupts, her eyes bright with interest.

"But as for now, will ye' have dinner with us?" I ask.

Patrick's eyes narrow. "O'Rourke stays on the other side of the table. For his own safety."

"That seems like a wise choice," Morana says, "Aisling, come over and meet my sister-in-law, Mala." She gracefully draws away Patrick's wife, who's still staring at a gloating O'Rourke, her eyes alight like the fires of hell.

Morana...

"Well, that was interesting," I say, stepping out of my high heels with a sigh of relief. It's been four months since I was shot, and it's a miracle I've kept Cameron from carrying me around everywhere. I could tell even my modest heels were causing him anxiety all night.

I was so happy to see that he'd re-booked us in the same suite we'd had before at the Clontarf Castle Hotel. There's a beautiful main room with a massive fireplace and even on a warmer night like this, Dublin's chilly enough that the roaring fire feels wonderful. All the furniture is antique and the exquisitely carved wooden four-poster bed is gloriously sturdy, even for a man as large and vigorous as my husband.

"Aye," he agrees, "I'm meetin' with Patrick tomorrow to hear the rest of the story. That wife of his is a banshee, isn't she?"

"She seems like she has her reasons."

He's looking at me now and I pause unbuttoning my dress. His forest green eyes are darker now, carnal. "Have I mentioned, wife, how very beautiful ye' are, sweetly swollen with my child?"

"A few times today alone," I laugh, "but it's always nice to hear it from you."

"Would it ruin this romantic moment if I mentioned that looking at these luscious tits of yours is making me hard enough to pound nails?"

"Such a smooth talker." I can't really be offended because that filthy look in his eyes is so promising.

"Take your dress off," Cameron seats himself in the wingback chair by the fire, swirling a glass of scotch.

Flushing, I look down. He tells me I'm beautiful all the time, but I know my body is different at nearly seven months pregnant. My breasts are a cup size bigger and my nipples are so sensitive that even the soft material of my bra makes them hard.

"Let me see you, lass," his voice is a rumble now, like a jaguar.

He's so handsome. Almost absurdly handsome in a way that doesn't seem quite real. And now, with the smirk on his full lips and his glimmering eyes… Damn it. I'm wet.

Peeling off my violet silk dress, I fight the urge to cover my breasts.

"Now the scanties, lass. I want you naked."

The bra comes off, my undies end up around my ankles.

"Crawl over here."

The smug bastard spreads his legs, watching me crawl across the carpet to him. It does feel sexy, prowling after him on my hands and knees. I run my hands along his thighs, heading for the extremely promising bulge in his pants. Instead, I stifle a yelp when he hoists me up, first to straddle him and then he puts my knees on the arms of the chair. One hand holds me in place, gripping my ass while the fingers of the other spread my lips wide, his thumb rubbing lazily on my clitoris.

"So wet, tart, and sweet, my dirty, delicious girl," he purrs, burying his face in my pussy.

My spine snaps into an arch and I would have fallen in an ignominious heap without his hand holding me steady. His beard scratches against my acutely sensitive center, his tongue tickling against my clitoris as he slides two fingers inside me, pressing harshly against all the sensitive, secret spots I never knew existed before him. I come so quickly that it's embarrassing, tightening down on his fingers.

"Fuck," my gorgeous, diabolical husband groans, "I'm jealous of my own goddamn fingers, gettin' squeezed so good." Gently moving my knees to straddle his hips again, he opens his pants, pulling out his shaft. "Hold onto me, lass." He kisses me and shoves inside me powerfully, invading me, spreading me wide, stretching me past the point of pain. He shoves his cock harder and shoves again until he's inside me deep, deeper than I've ever felt him, his hips pressed against my spread thighs.

"Here's what I want you to do, my filthy girl," he whispers in my ear, biting my lobe. "You're going to squeeze that tight little ass of yours hard. Strangle my cock. Squeeze it. If you don't make me come fast, I'm going to make this last for *hours*."

I don't know if that's a threat. I think it sounds very promising.

He grips my waist and begins moving me up and down, bouncing on his cock as his mouth stays buried between my breasts. My hands slide into his hair, nails digging into his scalp helplessly. I can feel myself tighten down on him, that damned piercing at the base of him is rubbing hard against my clitoris and I can't stop it.

"I'm sorry, I'm sorry!" I moan, "I can't wait."

"Don't you dare come!" he snarls, "Hold it."

"No," I moan, "it's too good."

He's fighting, he's holding back but he started it with that piercing, so I reach back and grip his balls, stroking them, using the slick soaking us both to roll them in my fingers and it's over. My dark husband roars, tendons tightening in his throat as he fills me, coming inside me until it drips out between us.

Burying my face between his neck and shoulder, I try to catch my breath. We're both coated in a sheen of sweat from the fireplace and the slick and come from us both is covering my ass and thighs.

Gripping a fistful of my hair, he pulls my head back and kisses me soundly. "You beautiful, wicked thing," he groans.

Lifting me off him like I'm no heavier than his glass of scotch, Cameron carries me into the bathroom. My favorite part of this suite is the magnificent claw-foot tub. As he fills it, he holds me steady as I list to the right, barely able to keep my eyes open. He piles my hair on top of my head, helping me into the tub and slipping behind me.

"When I tried to imagine my future," I mumble, "I could never see anything. Nothing solid. It was always dark."

"And now?" Cameron asks, his long fingers idly circling my nipples.

"It feels like more happiness than I deserve," I admit. "You gave me a life. A family. A baby."

"You deserve everything," he says, kissing my hand, kissing my wedding ring, and then the thin skin of my wrist. He chuckles as I shiver.

"There's one thing I just can't figure out," I muse.

"Which is?"

"What is going to be our 'meet cute'? What are we going to say to this baby when one day, they ask how we met? I don't feel like the kidnapping thing is going to present the best example of courtship."

His broad chest is shaking as he smothers his laughter.

"This isn't funny!" I smack his wet bicep, admiring the golden eyes of the dragon tattoo coiling around the muscle as they glare back at me.

"How about... once upon a time, there was a beautiful princess trapped in a tower-"

"It was a two-story dressing room."

"Who was rescued by a handsome prince-"

"Who threw her out of said two-story window."

"Then carried her off on his white horse-"

"A floral delivery van that got a flat."

"And they lived happily ever after."

We sit in silence for a moment, swishing the warm water. "That last part is pretty good," I agree.

Kissing the top of my head, my beautiful husband says, "We'll work on the rest."

What happens next with Cameron and Morana? Does the legendary Ivanov misfortune continue? Read on for a look into their lives, a few weeks later in the extended epilogue.

A FAVOR, PLEASE?

If you enjoyed the adventures of Cameron and Morana, could I ask you to leave a starred rating or perhaps even a review? Reviews and ratings are the lifeblood of an independently published book and can mean the difference between success and failure.

Even just a couple of lines about something you enjoyed in the book would mean a great deal.

Don't forget to the read the extended epilogue for Cameron and Morana here. dl.bookfunnel.com/z93xfz20y6

Cameron's brother Dougal showed his savage side in the showdown with the human traffickers. But what happens when something is stolen from him? Something very rare and valuable, by a very beautiful, cunning enemy. Dougal is pissed off and not in the mood to be a gentlemen. Read his story Illicit - A Dark Scottish Mafia Romance, live on Amazon on May 3rd, 2024

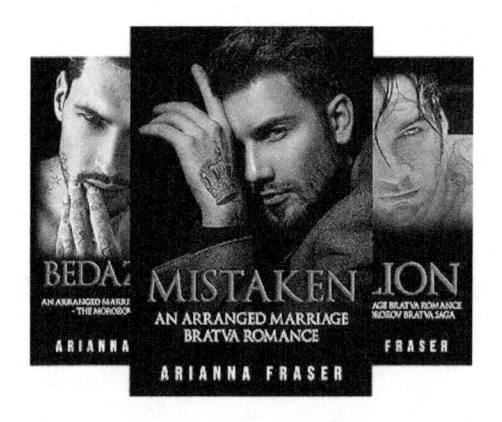

If you're curious about the backstory of Patrick and Aisling Doyle and the mysterious, super-hot and sociopathic billionaire Nolan O'Rourke, it all begins with the Morozov Bratva Saga, which can be found here: bit.ly/3TN9eSs

BOOKS BY ARIANNA FRASER

All available on Amazon

Arranged Marriage Bratva Romance
Mistaken - Book One of the Morozov Bratva Saga
Bedazzled - Book Two of the Morozov Bratva Saga
Hellion - Book Three of the Morozov Bratva Saga

The MacTavish Stolen Brides Series
Relentless - An Arranged Marriage Mafia Romance
Illicit - A Dark Scottish Mafia Romance

The Ares Academy Series
Lethal - A Dark College Bratva Romance
Malice - A Dark College Bratva Romance
Perilous - A Dark College Mafia Romance

Arranged Marriage Mafia Romance
Deceptive - Book One of the Toscano Mafia Saga
Deconstructed - Book Two of the Toscano Mafia Saga

Forced Marriage Mafia Romance:
Tales from the Corporation Series
The Reluctant Bride - A Dark Mafia Romace
The Reluctant Spy - A Dark Mafia Romance
Mr. and Mrs. Ari Levinsky Invite You to... the Worst Wedding Ever

Dark Vampire Romance
Blood Brother - Captive Blood One
The Birdcage - Captive Blood Two

Loki - Norse Mythology
I Love the Way You Lie -
Loki, The God of Lies and Mischief: A Dark Romance

FREE BOOKS!

Join my email list and I'll shamelessly bribe you with free books. You can start by downloading your copy of The Reluctant Spy - A Dark Mafia Romance here.
dl.bookfunnel.com/6xud62rmg0

I'm too lazy to spam you, so you'll only see an email for giveaways and new releases like Illicit - A Dark Scottish Mafia Romance, live on Amazon on May 3, 2024.

ABOUT THE AUTHOR

Arianna Fraser

Working as an entertainment reporter gives Arianna Fraser plenty of fuel for her imagination when writing romance-suspense stories. There will always be an infuriatingly stubborn heroine, an unfairly handsome and cunning hero - or anti-hero - romance, shameless smut, danger, and something will inevitably explode or catch on fire. She is a terrible firebug, and her husband has six fire extinguishers stashed throughout the house. She is also very fond of snakes.

When she's not interviewing superheroes and villains, Arianna lives in the western US with her twin boys, obstreperous little daughter, and sleep-deprived husband.

Have something to share? arianna@ariannafraser.com

Let's be friends:
TikTok - https://www.tiktok.com/@author.arianna.fraser
Instagram - https://www.instagram.com/authorariannafraser/
Bookbub - https://www.bookbub.com/profile/arianna-fraser
Pinterest - https://www.pinterest.com/AuthorAriannaFraser/
Tumblr - https://www.tumblr.com/ariannafraserwrites
Goodreads - https://www.goodreads.com/author/show/19264789.Arianna_Fraser